DARKEST
VI CARTER

WARNING

This book is a dark romance. This book contains scenes that may be triggering to some readers and should be read by those only 18 or older.

NEWSLETTER

Join my newsletter and never miss a new release or giveaway.

*Scan the QR code to
sign up.*

CHAPTER ONE

SCARLETT

Hunger can make us turn feral. Uncontrollable. I've made some pretty bad decisions while hungry. I've done things I'm not proud of for food. My stomach roars, and I tuck my chin into my chest as I walk down the main street. All's quiet at this time of the morning. A park beside the store has a few people jogging or out for an early morning walk. They look healthy and happy. *I hate them.* The warmth from the overhead heater blasts me as I enter the shop. The heat is enough to make me want to curl up under it and go to sleep. My bones ache like I'm eighty instead of twenty-one.

I stop, inhaling a deep breath. The scent of freshly made breakfast rolls wafts from the deli. My stomach gives another savage roar.

Don't linger, Scar. Just get what you need and get out.

My gaze roams over all the food. I want it all. I try to focus and not look so jumpy. Everything calls to me. My dirty sneakers shuffle forward and I'm standing in front of rows of colorful wrappers. My hands become clammy inside the wool gloves. The wool was once pink, now I can't really put a name to the color. Maybe grayish-pink.

My fingers wrap around the Mars Bar and my stomach roars again. It's too loud. A man glares at me. He doesn't look like an assistant; he looks like he owns the shop. He shakes his head slightly, telling me not to do it. My clothes tell the story of my homelessness. My long, unkempt hair is giving away my lack of money. I should put it back. Tears sting my eyes as I think of replacing the bar and going hungry.

It's a snap decision. My fingers tighten around the bar and I spin, tearing from the shop.

"Stop!"

I run faster and hit the door hard, nearly toppling over a woman pushing a pram. I want to apologize but the shop owner is right behind me. He lunges for me, but I skip away from his grasp and run out onto the road. A car horn beeps, making my heart race. The car screeches to a stop and I slam my hands on the bonnet. I meet the angry eyes of the driver before I continue running across the street.

"Come back!"

The shop owner is right behind me. *Oh, shit.* My feet hit last night's rainfall as I run down the alleyway. The moment I become aware of my surroundings, I know I'm caught. The alleyway cuts off—it's a dead end. A ladder attached to the building to my left hangs down close to the ground. I clutch my candy and race for it.

"Stop!" The shop owner's shouts make my thin legs move quicker. I grab the rung of the ladder and pull myself up. The rungs disappear under me as I scale the ladder quickly, and when I look down, he's glaring up at me with a promise in his eyes.

I fucked up. I know I did. My eyes water as I clear the ladder and roll onto the rooftop, landing on my back. My heart races a million miles an hour. I sit up and grip the brickwork and shuffle forward so I can peer back over the edge. He's no longer below me—he races back across the street. I don't take my focus off him until he turns and glares back up at the rooftop; I duck my head. I don't linger, but start to make my way across the building. A small wall separates the next roof. I cross the wall and grin. My stomach growls and I wrap my arms around my abdomen. I'm ready to sit down and start eating.

Everything in me stills as my vision zeroes in on a man lying flat on his stomach on the next rooftop over. I move forward, trying to get a better look at him. He's so still. He's dead. My stomach sours further.

Leave him, Scar.

My feet move quietly towards him. The saliva in my mouth dries up as I get closer. He's dead. Oh, God. I need to tell someone. Why is he up here? Maybe to sleep? There are a lot of homeless people in Dublin, far more than there should be. I chew my cracked and dry lips until a metallic taste fills my mouth. I stop moving as my gaze hones in on a long black rifle that's lying against his shoulder. Fear shoots through me as I continue to study the man. His head moves ever so slightly, his eye against the scope. The movement causes my heart to skyrocket and fear buzzes and rattles in my bones. I need to leave. He's not dead. I need to leave now.

The rifle aims out towards the park. Bile crawls up my throat.

Go, Scar.

A man jogs in the park. He's oblivious to the shooter who has trained his rifle on him. The shooter shifts slightly, rolling his shoulder as he moves his finger to the trigger.

He pulls the trigger.

The click is soft, but it's like a punch to my stomach as the jogger falls to the ground. People around him stop, and a woman starts to scream. More people come over with hesitation in their steps to see why she is screaming. There's a lot of commotion and crimson liquid leaves the jogger's head.

I swallow more bile. The shooter's dark eyes connect with me and I'm ready to throw up. The rooftop disappears quickly as I run for my life. I know he's chasing me from the shift in the space behind me. He isn't making much noise but he's there. I won't look back, I want to so badly but I need to focus. I clear another wall and jump. I have no idea what I will land on. I hit the surface and feel a burning in my ankle, but I don't slow down. The heavy thud has me looking back. He's cleared the wall. His eyes are filled with violence that he will unleash on me if I get caught. I jump from one building to the next. The gap is small but my body hits the new rooftop hard. It knocks the air from my lungs. I scramble back up and fall sideways, my body giving up on me. A hand grabs my shoulder and spins me mid-fall. I tumble to the ground and I'm staring into the barrel of a gun.

My hand moves slowly into my pocket, where I left my bar. I can't let it go. I can't lose it. It's stupid that I'm thinking about the food when I'm about to die. But in case I somehow survive this, I'll have food.

"What are you doing up here, little girl?"

Little girl? I take another look at the man, but my fear makes everything buzzy and fuzzy.

The tip of the rifle is cold as he presses it against my cheek. "Answer the fucking question."

"I was hiding."

His eyes dart to my pocket that I still have my hand in. "What's in your pocket?"

I'm shaking my head. He can't have my candy. I'll starve. My logic has left me and I can't reason with the madness right now.

"Take your hand out of your pocket slowly, or I'll pull the trigger."

The hairs rise on the back of my neck. My heart is ready to leap from my body and nose-dive off the side of the building. Maybe running and jumping would be better than being shot up here. How long would it take for anyone to find me? I have no one who would look for me. Would anybody care? I look longingly at the edge.

The man cocks the gun and my attention is drawn back to him. As I slowly remove my hand from my pocket, he moves back slightly, but I can see in his eyes that he is ready to pull the trigger. My vision wavers as I slowly hold out the Mars Bar. His gun points at the candy. I blink and tears spill as I open my fingers. The bar is squashed. I'm sure it's also melted from the sweat that soaks my hand. I'll still eat it if I live long enough.

A half cry bubbles from my lips. The man's dark eyes focus on my face.

"Who are you hiding from, little girl?" He holds the gun to my head again.

Tiredness rattles my bones and I let my eyelids flutter closed. I tighten my hold on my prize. "The shopkeeper."

"Open your eyes." The barrel of the rifle presses into my cheek. The cold steel has me alert and my heart starts a new rhythm of fear.

"I saw nothing," I plead, not ready to die.

"You stole that bar?" His eyes go to my candy and I pull it close to my chest. My stomach roars again. I just want to eat it. I think of asking him if

I can have the bar before he pulls the trigger. Let me die with something in my stomach.

"Can I eat it?" I ask.

His eyes darken. Half his face is covered in black hair. His beard is thick and I wonder if food ever gets stuck in all that hair.

He takes a step closer and my eyelids squeeze together. This is it. Not how I expected my life to end. I thought I would starve to death in an alleyway or be mugged for my pitiful belongings. My hand reaches for my neck where the one and only possession I have hangs. I don't get to touch, I don't get to run my fingers across the pendant one more time.

Pain explodes behind my lids and burns my face. My stomach roils and the world tilts as I hit the ground. I can't see. My skull is on fire. Is this what death is? No images flash before my eyes. I blink and the last thing I see is large military boots before the world drags me to the pit of hell.

CHAPTER TWO

SCARLETT

My head aches. The first thing I'm aware of is the smell. It's different from the scent of the city and rainfall. It doesn't all smell of cold steel. It's warm, manly-cologne. God, it's been so long since I inhaled anything so nice. My stomach shifts, and I groan to hold down the bile in my stomach. I open one eye first. A beige, shaggy rug is under me. My fingers immediately separate as I sink them into the fibers to try to keep myself from spewing everywhere. I open my other eye and the room comes into focus. I'm in a living space. Four short legs of a coffee table are in front of me. A black leather couch is beyond that. The cushions on the couch are the same beige as the rug under my hands. My gaze skitters to the ceiling where pin lights shine down on me. I close my eyes as a new wave of pain assaults my head. Hairs rise on the back of my neck as footsteps ring out close to me. A wave of dizziness sends the room into a spin. I know I shouldn't move, but I slowly draw my legs up to my chest.

"I know you're awake."

My eyes pop open, my heart threatens to explode from my chest. What will he do to me? He killed that man without hesitating. A whimper pulls from my lips.

He bends down and places a finger over his lips. "Shhh."

I want to close my eyes, I want to disappear, but I fear if I blink that he'll hurt me. My jaw feels like it's being wound up too tightly, like it might shatter at any moment.

His dark eyes roam across my face. My heart beat thrashes in my ears and I can no longer hear any other sound. Even as he stands back up—it's soundless. He turns and leaves me, my fingers tighten around the shaggy rug. He's going to get his gun, he's going to end me now. I never had my Mars bar. I swallow the bile that rises in my throat again. Over the pounding of my heart I can make out the sound of running water. My gaze darts around the room for a weapon. A large red and black lamp sits on a table beside the couch. I could use the lamp, I could hit him with the brass end.

The water stops running. My hands dig further into the rug.

Move, Scar.

If I get the lamp, I can hit him over the head and escape. I'm playing out my next move in my head, but my body won't move. I'm afraid to move. He returns, holding a glass of water that he has no doubt laced with poison. He kneels down and like I'm some dog and he pushes it close to my lips. "Drink." His words are sharp.

The glass clangs against my teeth as I attempt to keep my cracked lips pressed together. A whimper slips from my open mouth as he pours the water in. My throat works by automatically swallowing and consuming what he gives. The cold water travels right down to my aching and empty stomach. He pulls the glass back and stares down at me.

"I don't want you to speak." He nods after his words.

The water in my stomach rebels and I try to focus on his face, focus on something so the liquid doesn't come up.

"I'm not sure what I'm doing with you yet, but this is my home. No one will ever find you. You need to resign yourself to that fact. You will never leave."

I swallow more bile. His mouth moves again but my heartbeat takes over my hearing. It rushes blood too fast through my body and the corner of my vision fades. If I were standing, I wouldn't be able to keep upright. I take a breath in through my nose and slowly let it out through my mouth.

His lips stop moving and fear chokes me. The glass is pushed against my lips again and he pours the remainder of the water into my mouth. My stomach quivers when the water hits it.

"You look like a Kate. So that's your name. That's what you answer to. Nod if you understand."

What? I'm bobbing my head.

"Do you want more water?"

I swallow more saliva that pools in my mouth, and nod.

He seems pleased as he rises and leaves me. My gaze snaps to the lamp again. It's a weird moment, a moment of clarity. I've been kidnapped and I am now this man's prisoner.

I shift my hand and it's all I need. I rise and the room tilts. I hear the running water as I crawl over to the table. *The lamp, just focus on the lamp.* That's all that matters, the lamp. With shaking hands I reach for the lamp and slowly take it down off the table. It's attached to a plug in the floor. I unplug it and wait. The water isn't running. I hear his footsteps returning to me. His feet appear.

"What are you doing?"

I slowly look up at him and stand as my insides sway. I can't stop the liquid that rushes up my throat as I spew the contents across his boots. He jumps back, the glass falls from his fingers and shatters across the wooden floor. I'm moving towards him as my eyes burn from getting sick. The lamp is so heavy, it feels like it's made of marble. I raise it with both hands and with every bit of strength I possess, I slam it down on his head. He stares at me with wide eyes briefly stunned as I bring the lamp down again. Blood runs down the side of his face and my stomach roils.

I'm waiting for him to fall over from the blow, but he continues to stare at me.

Run, Scar.

The bang of the lamp when it hits the ground has me running across the wooden floor, which changes to a hard marble flooring. I pass a kitchen and move down a long white corridor. He isn't following me. I turn each door handle, trying to find a way to the outside world. Each door has my pulse spiking: bedroom, bathroom, a gym, a living space. The last door I open, I pause. The walls are decorated with guns from floor to ceiling. I've never held a gun in my life, never mind fired one.

"Kate!"

My body locks up as he calls my name. My legs refuse to move as cold air creeps over me. I want to curl up—or let him get me—so this ends.

"Kate!"

The sound of my name leaving his lips is the key that unlocks me and I grab a gun off the wall. He enters the room and I spin, holding it up.

"I'll shoot." Tears leak from my eyes as I speak.

He holds up both hands and pauses in the doorway. The gun must be loaded. I blink and more tears fall. "Move into the room."

He takes a step towards the wall.

"The other side!" My hands tremble and I try to steady the gun. He listens to me and moves to the other side of the room with his hands still in the air.

He takes a step towards me.

"Stop!" My stomach roils and I swallow the sick this time. "You stay back." I warn him.

He pauses. Blood still runs from the side of his face. *I don't want to hurt anyone. I just want to leave.*

"Don't move." I remind him as I walk backwards toward the door. "Don't follow me." I add.

My words have a calming effect on me. They're telling me I'm in control and I will survive this. That it's okay. This is a blip in my messed up life.

He takes a step towards me and when he lowers his hands, I hold the gun higher.

"I will shoot you." I plead with my words for him not to make me become a killer. He takes another step and tears leak from my eyes.

"Please!" He keeps walking and he's going to reach me and kill me, I see the brutality in his eyes.

My eyelids flutter closed as I pull the trigger. The snap has me opening my eyes. It should have been a bang, not a snap. My eyes clash with his and I keep pulling the trigger; each time fear consumes me. The gun's empty. His dark eyes tell me he already knew that.

He reaches me and pulls the gun from my hand. It hits the ground hard and sails across the wooden floor. Heavy hands grab my arms and I'm airborne, my head hits his back as he slings me over his shoulder. I'm frozen as the world blurs around me. The pendant on my necklace swings in front of my face like a pendulum. My fists hit his back as he carries me further down the white corridor.

"No!" I keep pounding my fists on his back and wriggling, but he doesn't stop or react. The upside down world blurs and rights itself as he releases me and I land on something soft. I bounce a few times and try to regain my balance. I don't have a second to process anything as steel wraps around my wrists. I yank my arms back and kick out at him, but he clamps the chains around the steel bed frame. My arms are stretched above me as I pull, fear claws its way up my throat.

I'm trapped.

I'm facedown on the bed. He rams my face into the blankets and for a moment it's like being underwater. The small sounds around me are amplified. He pushes down on my head a few times, I think he's shaking me. I close my eyes and try to go someplace else. I've been here before. This place of darkness—but it's quiet.

The darkness shatters as his hand grips the back of my neck, the sound rushes back in as he forces my body deeper into the bed. The heaviness of his body has my chest tightening. His erection brushes against my ass and the air stills in my lungs.

He's going to rape me.

"Nooo!" I buck my body while I scream, spit and shout. I can't control the absolute terror that assaults me. "Nooo!"

I'm screaming. He's shouting and I can't silence the fear in me. My head is pushed down into the bed again. His breath is quick against my ear.

"Shut up." His words are like a gunshot that pierce through my veil of terror. "Just shut up." He's breathing heavily and I want to leave this place. A sob tears from me and he rams my head into the blanket one final time before the bed creaks and the weight of him vanishes. The slam of the door has more tears falling, as I cling to the quilts and try to find an anchor to hold me together. The air grows thinner. I sit up as far as my restraints will allow. My hair is plastered to the side of my sweaty and tear soaked face. He's gone. My eyes confirm what my mind had already told me. I'm alone. I want to scream. I want to lash out. I want my freedom. Turning my head into my arm I sink my teeth into my jacket, it penetrates all the way to my flesh. The pain is instant and registers with me, I sink my teeth deeper until that's all I am, one huge ball of pain. I release my burning skin. My pulse pounds in my gums as I yank my arm. I fall slightly back as the cuffs come away from the bed. A small gap at the top of the steel bar has allowed them to slip through. I'm staring at my hands, wondering if I've passed out and I'm dreaming. I quickly stand and push my hair out of my face with my joined hands.

The door handle is heavy as I wrap my trembling fingers around the cool steel and I push down on it. The click of the door is like a gunshot. He never locked the door. Hope blossoms inside me. I can escape.

CHAPTER THREE

DEAN

I shift my rock hard cock as I leave her. My heart pulsates rapidly. I
never thought my adrenaline could reach such heights. Even when
I lay on the ground and take a kill shot. Nothing felt more exhilarating
than when she pulled that gun on me. One bullet, that's all it takes to
end a life. One pull of the trigger and it's all over.

She pulled the trigger; Kate has balls. I'd give her that, but her fear
tastes delicious. My cock grows harder, but the pain in my head wins
my attention as I step into the weapons room. Bending down, I pick
up the 9mm and place it back on the wall. I grin as she moves past the
door quietly like I might not hear her. There is no way out of here.
She'll learn that soon. We are underground in my safe house. No one
knows where I live. I have to live like this, too many want me dead.

"Kate," I say, as I step away from the wall. I fix my erection. I'm surprised at my reaction to her. She looks like a kid, she smells bad too, but her body has curves and dips that tell me under all that—she's a woman. One I clearly want to fuck. It's her eyes, crystal clear and filled with so much fucking fear.

"Kate," I sing again as I step out into the hall. I hear the rattle of the drawers in the kitchen.

Fuck.

My head throbs again, a reminder of what she did to me.

"You can't get out. If you hurt me again... I will punish you." A part of me hopes she does, I want to punish her. I know I should have killed her, keeping her is wrong. But no one knows she is here. She will never leave. I can do whatever I want and no one can judge me. Only she can.

I decide that Kate is not judgmental, that she is actually very open-minded and understands that she brought this upon herself. I step into the kitchen and I can't see her. A towel is on the counter, I pick it up and press it to my head.

"Kate!" I duck as a carving knife jabs towards me. The little bitch. I keep ducked down along the counter and listen. She's on the other side, breathing heavily. Her fear causes the blood to pump too fast around her body.

I slam my fist against the counter and she screams.

"I like you, Kate. Maybe that's why I didn't kill you." I speak and remain silent for a moment before I move around the counter. I pounce, stealing the element of surprise. She's holding a knife and arcs it towards me through the air. She's too slow, I knock it from her hands and watch as her eyes widen with pure fear that I drink up. She shuffles back against the cupboard like she might dissolve into it.

"You like me chasing you?" I hunker closer to her and she presses a tear-soaked cheek into the cupboard door.

Her fear emanates from her and I inhale it along with the undertone of an unwashed body.

"Get up."

She whimpers again like a puppy.

"Kate." I warn and she looks at me. "Get up."

She does slowly, the tremble in her hands rattle the chains around her wrists.

"Walk." I step aside and she moves; as she passes me she hunches her shoulders like I might deliver a blow. "We aren't all violent like you, Kate," I say.

She keeps glancing at me over her shoulder. "Keep walking." The warm blood on the side of my face continues to trickle. I'm aware of the path I'm leaving behind on my clean wooden floors.

"Take a left."

She stalls. I'm ready to issue a warning when she opens the bathroom door.

I'm intrigued to see what's under all these clothes. I also want the smell of her dirty body out of my home.

She stops and spins around. Her face has lost all color as I step up to her. She shrinks under my stare. She's already small, but now she reminds me of a kid. I hate that. The moment I take the handcuffs off her, she rubs her wrists.

"Take off your clothes."

Her gaze snaps up to me and her eyes fill with a fresh kind of terror. A part of me wants to become the monster she fears. I want to strip off any morals of right and wrong and take what I want. She opens the buttons of her green army jacket.

"Kate, I'm aging here. Speed it up."

Her cracked lips tremble as she peels off the jacket that's going straight into the fire. The more fabric that's removed, the more I pity her. She doesn't understand I will have to kill her. But, for now, I will continue to give her hope. Let her think she might live. Otherwise, this won't be fun. She's trying to cover herself as she stands in front of me in off-white underwear and a bra.

I glare at her and she unfolds her arms and reaches back, unclasping the bra. She has bigger breasts than I expected. She's curvy, but I felt them through her clothes. Her skin is surprisingly clean—no blemishes. Her cheeks burn with heat as she removes her underpants. She stares at the wall and refuses to meet my eyes. I step away from her and walk into the shower. Turning on the dials, I check the temperature.

She's still standing, staring at the wall when I step out of the shower.

"Get in." She hunches her shoulders as she walks past me, her head buries into her chest, like she might disappear. Her ass is perfect and my erection grows as she steps under the spray of water. The silver pendant is the only thing she wears as she stands still, allowing the water to assault the crown of her head.

Nobody knows she's here. I can take what I want. The thought has me stepping closer to the shower. The floor slopes in slightly. She glances at me over her shoulder, blinking rapidly to keep the water out of her terror-stricken eyes.

Her lips drag down at the corners, she has a perfect mouth. The longer she stands under the spray of water, the more attractive she's becoming. It's like finding something buried in the earth. Each drop is washing away the thick layer of dirt. Her hair is a lighter brown, even under the water. The strands fall down to the middle of her slim back. The pulse in her neck pounds alongside a vein that's growing more prominent.

I step back out and her stiff frame falls forward slightly. I take a step towards her and her eyes grow insanely big.

I stop playing with her and let her wash. Going to the cupboard, I take out shampoo and body wash and return with them.

"Here, Kate." I hold them out and she stares at them for too long. "Take them." I warn.

She scurries forward and snaps them from my hands. The movement causes her breasts to bounce. Her nipples are so pink and I want to taste her. My eyes move across her flat abdomen before rising back up to her eyes. Her stomach rumbles and it reminds me of the Mars Bar. She was starving then—and that was hours ago.

I leave the room, not giving her an explanation but keep the door open. No doubt she will scurry around looking for something to hurt me with. I touch my head that still bleeds slightly. I have to avoid the droplets of blood on my floor as I walk back to the kitchen. Her aim was excellent. I gather up all the knives and anything else she might try to kill me with. Wrapping them all in a towel, I tuck it under my arm before grabbing the first aid kit from the drawer and making my way back down to the bathroom. I stop at the laundry room and place the towel with the knives into the dryer.

"I hope you're finished, Kate," I say before entering. She's still in the shower, her back is to me. She's hunched over whatever is in front of her.

"What are you doing?" Her hands are moving continuously. When I step closer, I see her hands are foamed up from the body wash.

"That goes on your body," I say as my eyes drink up all that flesh. I step in closer to her, she glances at me and she's quicker than I could expect. Her hands reach for my face as she tries to cover my eyes with the body wash. I easily grab both her hands and I can't stop the laugh that tears from me. Her face tenses and the tremble in her body ripples across her flesh before I push her back into the stream of water. I don't care that I'm getting soaked. Blood drips from the side of my face onto her breasts, breasts that I can't stop looking at. I push her to the wall, slamming her back against it.

"You are hell bent on hurting me, Kate." I don't mind. She's making it fun. My gaze skims up to her mouth. My erection pushes against her stomach. She tries to turn her head away from me.

"Look at me."

Her eyes snap to mine, she's ready to say something. But I allow no one to judge me.

"Don't speak unless you want me to punish you."

Her mouth snaps shut. I want her to break my rule. I want to punish her. She's so much smaller under me. I bend my head and dip my face into her neck. She smells nice. The coconut body wash is heavy in the air. She must have used it all. I lean out and look at her again. She's beautiful and that mouth would look perfect around my cock.

"I should have killed you." She tests all my restraints. She's only been here a few hours and my mind hasn't left her for one second. All I want to do is fuck her.

My hand grips under her chin and I tighten my hold around her neck, pushing her head back so she looks up at me. "I should have ended your life."

It's so easy. The pressure from my finger on the trigger ends so many lives. I push her head further back until it connects with the shower tiles; the water continues to pound down on my back. My black clothing soaked,

19

my boots have filled up with water. The blood on her breasts grabs my attention.

A grin tugs at my lips. "You're turned on, Kate," I say as I dip my finger into the blood before circling it around her hard nipple. I flick it and her hand connects with my face. The impact has me releasing her neck. Her chest rises and falls rapidly as she stares at me in horror.

She's ready to speak and I don't tell her not to. Her lips form a tight line. My face fucking throbs. She hit me in the same place she had tried to bash my skull in.

"You're very fucking violent." I wince and step away from her. "Now I will have to punish you."

She's shaking her head and my anger has me tightening my fists. "Don't act so innocent. Look at my head."

I don't want to shout. I won't let her get to me. She is mine and I have total power here.

"I was going to give you clothes, but now I won't. So get out."

She doesn't move. "If I come back in there, Kate, I won't stop." She's moving quickly as she steps out of the shower and grabs a towel.

"Dry yourself and leave the towel here. I'll see you in the kitchen in five minutes."

I turn to leave the bathroom. "Don't make me come looking for you." I grin as I leave.

CHAPTER FOUR

SCARLETT

The chair is cold under me. I'm struggling to breathe. My chest feels too tight. I try to cover myself up by crossing my arms. The table is hiding my most intimate parts. He glances at me over his shoulder from the kitchen area. A white bandage on the side of his head looks stark against the inky color of his hair.

The grains of wood on the table become my focus as he walks towards me with a piping hot plate of food. The smell of scrambled eggs has my stomach somersaulting.

It's visually appealing as he slides the plate in front of me, before dropping the knife and fork that he has tucked in his hand. "Now, Kate, you try to hurt me with these..." He taps the utensils. "You will have to eat with your hands."

I quickly look at him and bob my head so he will go away. He's too close. He stands and my stomach rumbles. The butter melts into the toast, a pool of golden Heaven. I focus as he walks away, but he returns too quickly with a glass of water. I don't react.

My gaze snaps up to him as he drags the heavy wooden chair out across from me and sits down with his own food. His eyes are trained on me. I haven't unfolded my arms from my chest; I don't want to be exposed. He starts cutting away at his eggs and shovels a spoonful into his mouth.

"Eat, Kate." He points at my plate with his knife. How much damage could that knife do? My skin burns as I unfold my arms and his eyes roam across my bare chest. I focus on picking up the knife and fork. My hands tremble, but I manage to scoop some egg onto the fork. I eat the first few forkfuls slowly. Savoring the flavor, the hint of pepper among the egg is a perfect contrast. I cut up some toast to accompany my egg. It's warm, the butter mingles with the egg and it's all perfect. It's the first warm meal I've had in a long time. I want to sigh in bliss, only to remember where I am. He's watching me.

"There is no better compliment than someone eating your food." His words have the food souring in my stomach.

My abdomen heaves and I swallow to keep the food down.

"I think we should get to know each other." He shovels more food into his mouth, seemingly oblivious to my discomfort.

"I'm a sniper by trade."

I know he is, but to hear him confirm it has my bones quivering. He pauses and fear shoots through me like a bolt of lightning. His eyes tighten around the edges and I have no idea what I've done. I didn't speak. *Did I?*

"Keep eating, Kate."

This time, when the food enters my mouth, I don't taste it. He seems satisfied and continues talking.

"Where was I? Oh, yes. So, I have one sibling. He is a real-life bank robber."

The water helps wash down the food that's lodged itself in my throat. I've eaten too quickly. Sweat slowly makes a pathway down my spine and entwines with the cold drips of water from the ends of my wet hair.

"We haven't seen each other in a long time. Our professions have us either working or hiding." He pushes his plate in and I refold my arms slowly over my chest.

I freeze when I draw his attention. "Take that off your neck." He points at my chain.

My hand instantly goes to the pendant. I'm shaking my head. Not this. I can't remove it. Panic sizzles my nerves and I can't stop shaking my head.

"Take it off. You are Kate. Kate doesn't like jewelry."

I want to plead with him. He has taken so much from me already, not this. My hand tightens around the pendant and I close my eyes against the painful memories that play out in my mind.

His smile never left through it all. That's what I remember the most about my dad, his smile. His kindness. His resilience. He opens his hand and the light catches the silver love heart. Half of the heart is missing. He walks to me with that smile. Oh, God, that smile. "This is for you, Princess."

I take the gift and frown up at him. "It's a broken heart."

He sits down on the edge of my bed and opens his other hand. "It's half of my heart. I have the other half, it's not broken. I'm just giving you a piece of me."

"It's okay, Daddy. You need all your pieces." I had tried to push the heart back to him. He's sick, I'm not. He needs them all.

His smile is back on his face again, only this time it wobbles. "Daddy wants you to have it, Princess. So I'll always be with you." He doesn't hand it back to me but places it over my head. The little half heart rests on my pink nightdress, it looks so pretty.

"I love you, Princess."

"I love you too, Daddy."

"Take it off." My mind returns to the kitchen and he's standing over me. I blink and tears spill.

Use your words, Scar.

My mouth moves.

"Don't you dare speak." His angry words have my lips trembling, but I can't let go of my dad's last gift to me.

He yanks my hand away from the chain and without even blinking he rips the pendant from my neck, and it's like the final piece of my armor vanishes. What have I to live for? A horrible look of satisfaction fills his eyes and I can't stop the scream that tears from my throat. For a moment he looks stunned, as I lash out and strike him, pain tears through me as my heart starts to bleed again. I'm not speaking, I'm screaming. He spins me and pulls me into his chest where he restrains my arms.

"Stop it!" The command has my anger ceasing and I feel so heavy all of a sudden. My heart bounces around my chest and I close my eyes and try to hang onto something—the razor that I stashed in the tank of the toilet. I focus on the sharp blade, I could cut his face with it. I could cut my wrists with it. The thought has my eyes springing open. I try to get out of his arms but they tighten around me, his erection pressing against my ass.

"I won't let you go until you calm down, Kate." His words are harsh against my ear and I stop moving. This is my fault. I shouldn't have stolen that bar, maybe then I wouldn't have ended up on that roof and now in

24

the hands of this maniac. He steps away from me and I'm all too aware of the cold on my back. I'm too aware of my nakedness. My fingers search for the chain that I know isn't there. Another sob tears from me and I want to scream at the top of my lungs.

I don't move as I hear him tidy up. He doesn't speak to me and I don't dare move a muscle. I need to get out of here or I am going to die. My hair still drips down the front of my chest. I don't dry it, I am too afraid of what will happen if I spend too long in the bathroom. My mind keeps telling me any second he will rape me. It's in his eyes. He's toying with the idea.

My stomach twists painfully, but for the first time, it's not from starvation. The meal is still unsettled but I need the food to stay down. I need my strength. I need to get out of here.

"It's been a long day. It's time for bed." I try not to react to the closeness of his voice. He circles around me until he towers in front of me. My heart starts a new beat, it's one that's driven by fear. He moves closer and I have to tilt my head back to see him. My breathing is harsh as he reaches for my face. His dark eyes don't hide his want. I want to close my eyes when he raises his hand to my face and runs his thumb harshly across my lips.

"You need to understand that no one knows you are here. No one will ever find you and there is no way out."

The air grows thin in the room. His eyes drop down to my lips where he rests his thumb.

"No one can judge you, Kate. We can do whatever we want."

I swallow around the lump in my throat as dread curls around the base of my spine. I need to reinforce the walls of my safe room. I need to not let any light penetrate it. I'm quickly checking the walls for any gaps, any cracks.

The coldness seeps in as he steps away from me. "Time for bed."

My jaw feels so tight as I follow him. I need to remain calm and find my safe place in my mind. I need to leave this place—even for a short while.

He flicks on the light in his bedroom. The bed takes up so much of the room. The black silky sheets have me stepping back.

Be brave.

The hallway looks like a safe place. It beckons for me to come.

I jump as material lands at my feet. He's watching me. "You will sleep on the floor until you learn to behave yourself, Kate."

I glance at the pillow and blanket. His eyes roam my flesh and fear skitters along my bare skin. I sink to the floor and cover myself with the blanket. I'm hoping he leaves me, but he doesn't.

He sinks to his knees. "I think we need to go over the rules."

His hand reaches out and he touches my face again. His fingers dance across my lips.

"You can't leave. There's no way out." Black orbs fill my vision and I nod.

"If you hurt me again, Kate, I will punish you."

He leans in and I don't dare move a muscle as he sniffs me. "You are making this very hard on me."

I picture my safe room. It's so dark. Soundless.

"Maybe you can stay in my bed."

My eyes shoot open and I try not to scurry away from him, it takes everything in me not to move.

His hand grips my face. His head lowers to me and I can't breathe. Soft lips brush against mine, I don't expect the softness or the warmth. I don't react, but my mind doesn't go to the dark room and I don't know why. I tighten my hold on the blanket so I don't push him away. So I don't aggravate him. When I don't respond to his kiss, he moves away from me.

"You're not ready yet." He stands up. "Goodnight, Kate."

I lie back down as I try to control the pounding of my heart. My lips sting and my body is all too aware of that kiss. I didn't flee to my dark room and I don't know why. How come I'm not feeling repulsed by that kiss?

I tighten my eyes and force myself to remember the blade in the bathroom. To remember that he will hurt me, rape me, and most likely kill me. I need to get out of here. I just need to try to keep my emotions in check and once he eases up—even a tiny bit—I will find my way out of this madness.

CHAPTER FIVE

DEAN

She's still asleep. Her bare chest rises and falls in a peaceful rhythm. The blanket has shifted throughout the night and she looks glorious while naked on my floor. She groans and I don't want her to wake up; I don't want to see the accusation in her eyes. My cock grows hard watching her. She groans again and I get up and leave sleeping beauty on my bedroom floor.

My fingers work quickly, pulling off the bandage on the side of my head as I walk to the kitchen. It comes away with some of my hair stuck to it. Rolling up the bandage I throw it into the trash and pause at the drawer that holds her necklace. It's her property, the only piece she came with. Taking the chain out, I hold the jagged heart in my hand. The hearts surface reflects the light and I can't see any scratches or marks, she really took care of it. My finger rubs the back and I can feel the inscription. It's her name no doubt, or a message from whomever gave the chain to her. It could be a lover. My finger continues to stroke the back of the heart as I remember her being upset. She wanted it back. I let the necklace slide from my hand and place it back in the drawer.

I check on Kate again as I pass the bedroom. She's still asleep, the blankets have sunk down to her waist. Maybe they will be lower when I return. I shift my hard cock as I enter the gun room.

The click of the safe is loud in the empty room. Taking out the phone, I stand and switch it on. I'm surprised to see a missed call from Gage. He doesn't call much; we aren't exactly close. We share the same DNA, but that is pretty much it. Gage is two years older, but it always feels like we are generations apart.

"You rang? Does that mean our parents are dead?" I close the safe door.

"Our parents are fine. I know they would love to hear from you." His deep voice has me wanting this conversation over. I can hear the judgment at my career choice.

"You know I can't be seen walking around."

"A phone call would mean the world to them." Traffic beeps in the background.

"On your way to rob a bank?" I question, as I try to veer the conversation away from my lack of sonly behavior. I will never be the son they want. I have good parents, they just never understand me.

Gage dismisses my question. "I got a photo yesterday. I'm sending it through to you now." The phone shuffles and my phone bleeps. "Did you get it?"

I hold the phone away from my face and look at the image that's loading slowly. Being underground makes the signal slow. The image finally loads and I curse.

"Where did you get this?"

"It was sent to me. I can't trace the number but they want fifty G's or they are going to the cops."

I hold the phone away from my face again and glare at the image of me stuffing Kate into the back of my vehicle.

"Where are you now?" I ask.

"I'm where this photo was taken. I'm trying to see the vantage point it was taken from. There's an abandoned building across the road. I think whoever it was, was on the second floor."

I hear more traffic move past him. "I'll be with you shortly," I say.

"Okay." Gage hangs up and a sickening feeling wraps itself around me. Someone had been watching me. Or had someone been watching Kate? I don't like the question that it raises. *Who is Kate?* I'm not ready to answer that.

I leave the gunroom and pause at the doorway for the bedroom. She's sitting up, clutching the blanket to her chest. Her eyes are focused on the bed. Her neck rises like she's trying to get a better look. Maybe she is trying to see if I am still in it.

"Good morning."

She jerks at my voice and her gaze zones in on me. "I have to go out for a while." I speak as I step into the room.

Her knuckles are white from the grip she has on the blanket. My approach causes her to stiffen further. Lowering myself to my knees, I watch the pulse flicker in her neck. I want to touch it—such a powerful emotion.

"I have to go out for a while," I repeat, as I look at her. *Hope.* That's what I see shine in her eyes and I smile. My smile is slow and deliberate and I watch in glee as that hope shrivels up and dies in her stunning ocean eyes.

"I think you know that the guns have no ammunition in them. The knives have been removed and if you try anything else while I'm gone, Kate, I will punish you." I let my gaze roam across her chest that's covered with the blanket. "A serious punishment." I reinforce as I rise to my feet.

I don't want to leave her alone. I don't want to return to the outside world, I don't want a reminder that the world still moves around us.

I'm staring at her as she draws her knees to her chest. I want to take her with me, but that wouldn't be smart.

"I'll be gone a few hours. You have permission to make yourself some food and I wouldn't say no to you making me food." I smile at the thought of coming back to a nice meal. "It would make me very happy, Kate."

She's looking at me like I'm mad. I think we all are in a way. It just depends on how you view it.

I leave Kate to her thoughts and get what I need.

I glance over my shoulder before I punch in the code. The heavy metal door opens with a suction sound. I pull it with both hands behind me and once I hear the click, I know there is no way out. It gives me some comfort as I climb the steps and enter the living space of the house that keeps my existence hidden.

I sip a coffee as I stand outside the shop that sits across the road from the building that I took the shot from. I turn when I spot Gage to my left. I walk slowly into the nearby park. It doesn't take long for him to catch up with me. I glance at him. We look alike, only Gage doesn't have a beard, his face appears clean shaven. He pulls the collar of his gray jacket up around his neck. His dark eyes are heavy with an accusation.

"Say what you want to say," I speak before drinking more coffee that really tastes like piss. I know better than to buy coffee from a machine.

"You really kidnapped someone?"

Yeah, I don't blame him; this is a first for me. "She saw me shoot a guy."

Gage stops walking, causing me to stop. His black hair has grown out slightly and the length is showcased as he runs his hands through it. "You should have killed her then."

I nod and look away from him. "Yeah, I should have, but I didn't." I look back at him.

His brows are drawn together with the question I'm not fit to answer. "What are you keeping her for?"

I start to walk. "Did you get any leads?" I ask, instead of answering his question.

"Nothing. I can't trace the number it came from, but you will have to reach into your purse and pay. I don't want mam or dad getting wind of this. It would kill them."

"If they knew you robbed banks for a living, that would kill them too." I'm not listening to his judgmental bullshit.

"Yes, just like if they found out you're a sniper." His hand grips my shoulder and I stop walking again. "Pay the money and then get rid of her."

I nod. I would have to get rid of her eventually, but that doesn't solve this problem.

"You know if I pay, it won't stop; they will want more."

He nods in agreement. "I'll be there when we make the transaction."

"Where do we make it?" I ask.

"I'm sure I won't have to wait long for a text, but in the meantime you need to find out everything about this girl."

Dread pools in my stomach and I walk over to a bin and throw in the paper cup. We don't speak as two joggers move past us. The two women smile at us and giggle once they pass.

"She has no one," I say, turning back to Gage.

"Obviously she does." I hate the prick for being right. Some fucker was watching us. I don't think it was a fluke. They must know her. Maybe she has people who care about her.

I nod again as a man walks past us with a large black dog.

"Will you come home for Christmas?"

I haven't been home in three years. The more I'm away from people, the more I want to stay away. "I'll see." I give Gage the same answer I always do. "Will you?"

He looks surprised at my question. I suppose I never ask. "Yeah, I always do, Dean."

"Oh, fuck off using my name." I look away from him. He's pulling that big brother crap with the tone in his voice. I don't have to answer to anyone, especially not him.

"When I hear from our mystery blackmailer, I'll let you know. In the meantime, try to figure out as much about the girl as you can."

"There was nothing in the building?" I ask, feeling frustration claw at me. I run my hand along my beard.

"The butt of a fag."

"Can you get someone to analyze it?" I ask.

Gage stuffs his hands in his jacket pockets. "I don't have those kinds of contacts."

"Yet, you know a guy who burnt off your fingerprints."

Gage grins at me. "It was a surgeon and I got skin graft done."

I shrug. "You still know dodgy as fuck people."

"I'll ask around." Gage finally answers. We've walked the full circle around the park. I'm ready to get back to Kate. I'm picturing her making me food. Waiting for me to return.

"What are you smiling for?" Gage asks.

I didn't realize I was. "Nothing. Let me know if you hear anything." I finish off as we reach the mouth of the park. I don't say goodbye as I walk back to my car.

I hate the thought of having to question her. Her name is Kate, I remind myself as I climb into the car and slam the door behind me. I turn on the engine as the first sign of rain mists across the windshield.

I need to kill her. Keeping her isn't an option. The engine kicks to life and I pull away from the sidewalk and make my way back home, knowing I'm not going to kill her—I'm not fit to. If I was, I would have pulled the trigger up on that roof and disposed of her. Killing her was never an option. She isn't a contract or a means to an end. No one paid me to take her out. Where that leaves me, I'm not exactly sure.

CHAPTER SIX

SCARLETT

The moment he leaves, I'm scrambling. I hear the click of the door as I step into the hallway. The blanket is forgotten, it's left discarded on the bathroom floor. My steps are measured as I make my way slowly up to the kitchen. The beat of my heart is too loud in my ears. I can't think straight. All I can think about is freedom. All I can think about is getting away from this madness. The empty space has the realization that I am alone for the first time hitting me fully. With tears in my eyes, I swallow down my panic and try to think about my next move. The drawer comes away quickly in my hands in my haste to search for a weapon. The contents spill across the kitchen floor, the noise has panic and fear rising in me. Falling to my knees, I gather up the drawer's contents and my hand touches the silver pendant given to me by my father. This time my eyes burn and I can't stop the onslaught of emotions and tears. Tears stream down my cheeks, the salty liquid finds its way into my mouth and slowly soaks into my soul. I can't read the inscription on the back of the pendant, with my finger I move it back and forth over my name. Scarlett.

I have always hated the smell of a hospital. It seems to mold itself with his crooked smile. The white gown with small blue dots drained the remaining color from his face. I always tried to mentally prepare myself for what I would find on the other side of the door. I knew one day I would open that door and he would be gone. That fear that held me daily, finally cut the air off from entering my lungs. That day had so much more significance to me because it wasn't simply about losing my father, it was about losing my only friend, the only person who mattered to me in the world.

I wipe tears from my face using the back of my hand as I frantically try to put everything back in the drawer. Releasing my necklace is painful, my fingers remain tight around the heart, the jagged edges pushing into my flesh. The bite of the pain has me rising and putting the drawer back.

My feet slap against the wooden floor as I enter the gun room. I don't hesitate as I take a gun from the wall and aim it at the floor, my heart pounds as I pull the trigger. The click of the gun is loud in the space, replacing it back on the wall I take down another gun and repeat the process. Each click has my heart jumping around in my chest. Each click has my disappointment growing, and my hope for release dwindles by the second.

I leave the gun room and race to the bathroom. My hand dips into the tank and I pull out the razor blade and hold it tightly in my fingers. It's all I have. It is my only weapon. I can use it against him or I can use this against my own mind. I know deep down that no matter what, I won't survive this. He isn't going to let me go. I shiver now as the cold from the tiles beneath my bare feet penetrate my flesh. I think maybe the cold is rising quicker through my system because of the fear.

Fear of not knowing what is going to happen to me. I have no idea how long he will be gone and something is telling me I won't get this opportunity again. I won't find myself alone. I spend the next while moving from room-to-room searching for something I can use as a weapon. A gym. It feels like Christmas. The heavy equipment would do some serious damage. Walking over, I pick up what I think is called a dumbbell; it's heavy in my hands and I raise it slowly above my head before lowering it back down.

This will have to work, this will be my only chance of getting out of this place. I'm nervous as I take a final walk around the space. I notice there are no windows and the heavy metal door looks more like something you would see on a bank safe. My stomach twists painfully. I try not to think about how claustrophobic this all is. I have no idea how long he's been gone, but I know a lot of time has passed. My stomach rumbles and it reminds me of what he had said about wanting me to make him food. Should I? Should I make him food so he won't suspect anything later on, or is making him food making me look suspicious? My decision is made for me when the large metal door clicks open. I move as quickly as I possibly can back to the bedroom and get under the blanket.

"Kate!"

My breathing becomes labored as his raised voice crashes against my ears, the sound of footsteps has everything inside me hallowing. The moment he steps into the room, his angry dark eyes send more fear shooting through my system. I think of the dumbbell, I think of the razor, I think of every unloaded gun, but nothing seems to calm me as he steps fully into the room. His lips don't move but his eyes are questioning me. Part of me wants to remind him I'm not allowed to speak.

"What is your name?"

I'm shaking my head in total confusion. I know the answer, but once again his warning about me not speaking, leaves my tongue heavy in my mouth.

"What is your name?"

My fingers tighten around the blanket as I continue to shake my head. He kneels down, ripping the blanket from my clenched hands. I want to beg him not to hurt me, but all I can do is shake my head.

"If you don't say your name!" The warning has me tightening my eyes. My lips feel so dry as they part and I swallow the lump in my throat.

"Kate." I open my eyes, startled by the sound of my voice. His own eyes seem wider and it's a brief moment where we are just staring at each other. The room spins and I touch the bedroom floor to try to steady myself.

"Get up!" He's standing, holding the blanket as I rise naked. His hands grip my arms and my attention snaps to him again.

"What is your name?"

His voice has a calming note to it, but I'm shaking my head. I don't understand what game we are playing. If I say my real name, will he punish me?

I open my mouth to speak again and his hand clamps across it. "Don't speak." My body starts to tremble as he storms from the room. His anger is growing and forming around the space. I can almost see his anger pulsate. I reach up to touch my pendant around my neck, it's my comfort when times are bad. My fingers touch only my flesh and tears burn my eyes again.

"Fuck!"

His roar has me jumping and I swallow the trepidation that's making my limbs heavy. I need to act now. His anger is too much. I have no idea what he will do to me when he returns to the room. My feet leave damp footprints on the wooden floor. My hand keeps touching my neck, seeking comfort, as I try to move quietly down the hall. I don't dare look over my shoulder. I can hear him moving around in the kitchen area. My feet feel slippery under me and I try to keep my balance as black spots dance in front of my eyes.

"What are you doing?"

A scream rips from my throat and I'm running. His pounding footsteps behind me, has my fear tripling as I race into the gym. I dive close to the dumbbells. Without thinking, I pick up the dumbbell. He bends down to get me and I swing, my life depends on me making contact. It's a horrible feeling as it sails through the air, it's so close to his face, he moves back and as the dumbbell pulls back down to the ground, my grip slips and it falls from my slick fingers.

There is a moment where I feel the world is suspended into a state of silence and stillness and I want to stay here. The bubble pops and he grabs my arm and drags me to my feet.

I don't beg with my words but try to plead with my eyes. His eyes are the darkest I have ever seen. *Don't cry, Scarlett,* I tell myself as he drags me to the wall. He pushes me against it before releasing me. He walks away from me before returning. I'm waiting for a punch or a slap, but instead his lips slam against mine. I don't move under him as his erection presses against my abdomen. His lips leave mine and I'm holding my breath as he dips his face into my neck, his breath fans out across my collar bone.

"You keep trying to kill me, Kate."

He doesn't sound mad, and when he leans out and grabs my face, I see lust swirl in the depths of his dark eyes. I try to ignore the reaction my body seems to have to him each time he is close. It's wrong. This is wrong. I hold still as his fingers tighten on my chin.

"Who are you?" His words brush my cheek and I don't want to think about who I am. Right now, I think I'm just Kate, who's been taken by this guy, whose name I don't know.

He releases my chin abruptly and my spine straightens as his fingers graze my pussy.

His fingers work fast and he pushes two inside me. My whole body goes still and I have that odd feeling of wondering if this is really happening. He removes them and pushes them back in. His eyes haven't left my face.

"You're wet." His words are gleeful and the heat to my cheeks is instant. I want to apologize. Something is wrong with me. I shouldn't enjoy this. I shouldn't allow this. His fingers plunge back inside me and when a groan falls from my lips, I close my eyes against the ecstasy—and also the shame.

"I want you to look at me." His deep voice has me returning to those abysses that I'm drowning in. "Just feel it." His words sound so real. Like he really wants me to just feel, I push my body harder against the wall trying to get away from his prodding fingers. But there is no escaping him. He widens me, adding a third finger. His palm grazes my hard nipples and I groan against the pleasure that bubbles up inside me. His mouth covers mine and I groan into his lips as he moves his fingers faster, his thumb brushes my clit as his other hand works on my nipple. He rolls it with his thumb and forefinger. My nerves all fire at once and as he moves faster, I feel the climax—it's so close. His lips press harder against mine and I take a taste, responding to his kiss. It's all too much, not just for me, but it seems to allow something to release in him. His tongue fills my mouth. His hand leaves my nipple as he grips my face, his fingers don't stop plunging inside me and I rise on the tips of my toes and break the kiss as I ride high on the orgasm that tears through me. He holds my face and watches me cum all over his fingers. I close my eyes, cutting him off from something so private. The moment I cum, shame follows on its heels far too quickly.

I'm still breathing heavy and don't look at him as he removes his fingers from me.

"What's your name?" His question now is gentler and I look at him.

Some twisted part of me wants to tell him but I hold back the only thing I can. "My name is Kate."

CHAPTER SEVEN

DEAN

"**M**y name is Kate," She repeats it again and her voice is stronger and louder. She's still flushed from cumming and I can't look away from her. She's so defiant. Her lips are slightly parted, red, and swollen from our kisses. The first time I kissed her did something to me, and then she hadn't responded. Having her respond this time has left me hungry for more. Now I know how sweet she tastes, how warm and soft her lips really are. I can't understand this want that's tangled itself within me. I want to know her. I want her real name and now she refuses to give it to me.

I could always check the pendant. My eyes travel across her bare skin, my own need has my cock hardening and pushing painfully against my trousers. I can see her orgasm shine on her inner thigh. My gaze travels back up to her eyes. Ocean eyes that are on fire with an anger she's holding back.

I want her to tell me what's making her so angry. The fact I touched her, or the fact she wanted me to.

My body is craving her and I know how dangerous that is. "Get dressed," I say.

Her eyes widen briefly but she doesn't move. I can't keep my hands to myself if she's naked. It just won't work for me anymore and I'm not about forcing myself on someone. I've never had to. Women come and go easily, so why am I so taken with this one?

She doesn't move.

"Get dressed now or I'll have you pleasure me." The thought has my balls growing heavier but fear has her skittering past me. I wait a few beats as I try to control my want for her, before following her into the bedroom. She's wrapped a blanket around herself. I take out a t-shirt and jogging pants along with some socks and leave them on the bed.

"Get dressed and then come up to the kitchen." I can't look at her as I leave the room. The kitchen area is fine. The moment I had returned I had checked the drawer to make sure the pendant was still there, it was. It might be something I can use to get information from her. I need to be smart and try to push aside the admiration that is growing inside me for her rebellious nature. I never saw the dumbbell as a weapon until today. It's a room I will have to lock. I don't want to wake up in the middle of the night to her standing over me.

She enters the kitchen in my clothes and every cell in my body is aware that she looks good in my clothes. They are baggy and too long on her, but with her flushed cheeks and wide eyes, her innocence calls to me.

I want to say something, but when she looks at me, words fail. I make the sandwiches. The chair scrapes along the floor as she sits down. I glance at her and she's watching me. I turn before she sees the grin on my face. I have a feeling she's up to something.

Something like trying to think of a way to kill me. It really shouldn't excite me but it does. Is it the thought of it all ending in a second? I'm not sure. I bring the ham sandwiches to the table and slide hers across towards her. It stops close to the edge and she lifts her small hands from her lap. She looks so young, but I know what's under those clothes. She takes a bite, it's slow and I can tell she's holding back from gobbling it down.

"How long were you on the streets?"

She freezes while staring at the small bite she's taken out of the sandwich, she takes another before looking at me.

"A while." Her voice is so soft and low. I like the sound of it.

I exhale loudly and place my sandwich on my plate. My patience is dwindling quicker than it ever had. "How long is a while?"

"Five months." She answers quickly.

"Who gave you the pendant?" It isn't really important, but I need to know why she values the chain so much.

Her lids flutter closed but not before I catch a glimpse of the pain that shines out of them. "A friend," she mumbles into the sandwich before she takes another bite. I can tell she's no longer enjoying it. I get back up and get her a glass of water. I have an overpowering urge to touch her. Placing the glass beside her, I don't leave and she slowly looks up at me. I can't stop myself from reaching out and touching her face.

"His name?"

She moves and my hand shifts to her hair, holding her firm so she looks at me. Fire starts to burn in her eyes again and all I can think about is touching her. My arousal grows quickly and I want her to defy me so I can take what I really want.

"Robert." Her eyes swim with pain.

"A lover?" The jealousy is instant and I release her like she burned me. Keeping her isn't good. This isn't good. I return to my chair to put some distance between us. But it's not enough.

My fist slams down on the table. She screams and her water glass wobbles before spilling across the table.

"Eat your food!" I bark and she picks up the sandwich. I see the tremble in her hands as she eats quickly. What the fuck am I doing?

"Do you have any friends?" I ask her.

She looks up at me, her eyes blurring with unshed tears. "No."

"Do you have anyone?"

She blinks and tears spill before she looks away from me. "No." She bites the sandwich and starts to chew quickly as tears stream down her face.

I can't deal with her crying. I focus on cleaning up the spilled water and refilling her glass.

"Who's Robert?" I ask as I sit back down. She seems slightly more composed.

Her sandwich is gone.

"My father."

I get up and place the other half of my sandwich on her plate. "Is he dead?"

She looks up at me like I've struck her. Her chest rises and falls quickly. "Yes." Her word is filled with air and I see her pain so fucking clearly.

"Mother?" I keep digging as I move to more steady ground. I sit back down and she reels in everything and cuts me off. "What does it matter?"

I want to slam my fist down on the table again but I reach for my own control. I don't respond. She needs to remember who has the power here.

"I never knew her." She grits her teeth, and I'm not sure if it's at me or the idea she never knew her mother.

"Siblings?"

She shakes her head. The half of my sandwich still sits on the plate.

"Eat," I say and am satisfied when she picks it up and takes a bite. I wait patiently as she eats the sandwich. I want her to finish it before I continue.

When it's all gone she takes a drink of water, the glass trembles in her hand.

"Cousins, aunties, uncles?"

"I have an aunt. She raised me after my father died." How did she end up on the streets is what I want to know.

"She died a year ago." She adds.

Her hands sit back in her lap.

"What's your name?"

I see a flash of something in her eye. It looks like uncertainty.

"Kate."

I stand and walk away from her to the drawer. The drawer with the necklace. I know it's her name that's inscripted on the back of it. I could just read it and end this. My gaze slams into hers. I want her to tell me. I want her to say her name.

"Any boyfriends or friends on the streets?"

She cuts me off again, a tell tale sign, I'm picking up that she's uncomfortable about something.

"Something happened to you?" I'm moving towards her again. Her head snaps up and she's shaking it, but nothing can hide the look in her eyes. Someone hurt her.

"What happened?"

Her chest rises and falls and I want the clothes removed. I want to see her.

She shakes her head again like she has a fucking choice.

"You will tell me." I lean closer.

"Yes, something happened to me." She doesn't blink as she looks up at me. "Some fucking psycho took me." Her voices rises and I'm ready to ask who, I'm ready to fucking kill him. "He took me to his home, removed my clothes, made me wash in front of him, chained me to a bed only to let me break free." Her voice continues to rise and it's tinged with hysteria. "He won't let me go." Fear chokes her and I can't look away. "He's going to kill me. He's going to kill Kate!"

I snap and grab her, flinging her across my shoulder. She doesn't fight me like she did last time. Instead she keeps shouting her truths. "He took me, he took me and I know he will kill me."

She's lost her fucking mind. I dump her onto the bed and she doesn't stop. "He took my father's gift from me. That's all I had of him. You." She points at me. "Took it from me." Her angry words feel like they are latching onto me. I want to tell her to shut up. I don't want to hear her words.

"You can't judge me." I fire back as I grab two ties off the rack in my wardrobe.

When I turn to her, I see the anger in her eyes. Anger I want to crush. "I think you want me to punish you."

I move closer with the ties, her gaze jumps from them to me. She won't answer, now she decides to grow silent again. My body wants her and I can't understand the want I have for her. I'm not gentle as I tie her hands together. She hisses as I pull her to the bedpost, and with the other tie I wrap her hands around the post.

"That's too tight." Her words wobble. I want to hurt her so badly. I finish tying her and before I can do anything, I leave the room, slamming the door behind me. Trying to block out how she sees me. My fist hits the wall. My knuckles ache and I focus on that as I check my phone again. Nothing from Gage.

I lean my head against the wall as I try to regain some of the control that is slipping so easily through my fingers. Her scream has me staring at the bedroom door. She's screaming at the top of her lungs. It sounds like someone is hurting her but I know she's alone. The need to check on her has me returning to the kitchen where I pour myself a drink. What the fuck have I done?

I take another large gulp of brandy. I could drop her off on the street. I take another drink. I could leave her and she would never see me again. She wouldn't be able to pinpoint where I'm located. I empty the glass. She could do what? Resume her life on the streets with people who could hurt her.

The glass sails across the room and I laugh as I watch it shatter. Opening the drawer I take out the necklace. My finger traces the name on the back. Her name. Her identity.

End this now, I tell myself, before I get in any deeper. Before I fall so far that there is no return.

I let the necklace float back into the drawer and close it.

CHAPTER EIGHT

SCARLETT

I continue to scream until my throat begs me to stop. My roar ends on a whimper. I can't sort through everything that spins in my head. I gave myself to him freely. I wanted his touch. Yet, I am his prisoner. I hate how easily I submitted to him. How easily I handed that power over. How I craved to have his long fingers inside me. The memory of the look in his eyes as I was close to climaxing has heat scorching my chest. I feel the heat crawl up my neck before it spreads out across my cheeks.

I close my eyes trying to shy away from my next thought. It's the most deadly thought, and I haven't acknowledged it, but I had the thought the first moment he had turned and looked at me while I was on the roof. I had thought about how good looking he was. *I am attracted to him.*

The only similarity they have is that I never told them to stop. I said nothing. Fear and uncertainty had me frozen back then. But that isn't the case with what just happened now. It isn't fear or uncertainty that has me just closing my eyes and wanting his touch.

Old hands fill my vision and I hate it as my skin crawls. I never told him to stop. In my reasoning at the time, I thought that maybe if I didn't say it out loud—or to anyone—it wouldn't be real. Maybe if I closed my eyes, each touch would be erased after it happened.

Each time, he took so much from me. It wasn't about my flesh; it was trust; it was my voice; it was my inability to trust anyone ever again. I was always waiting for that blow of betrayal from a friend, or the control of a boyfriend. That's all I could understand. It made sense in my messed up mind. Maybe that's why I'm attracted to this guy...he didn't smile at me. He didn't pretend to *not* be a monster behind his painted mask. No, he just never wore a mask. He doesn't pretend. He *is* a monster.

Before, there was that one time, that one time that just became the final time. It was too much silence, too much of being stuck inside my own head and I broke free. I broke free by running.

You can't outrun yourself. I push away that voice that tries to laugh at me.

That's what had led me to live on the streets. Having nothing was so much better than having something for someone to take. He took, and kept taking, and I knew it would never stop. I still blame myself. If I had just said no that first time, or second or third or fifth, maybe, just maybe, it wouldn't have continued.

I yank my arms back from the bedpost only to cause a burn across my wrist. I want to scream again. I wish I wasn't allowed to speak; speaking to him is making this worse. It's making it more personal, and the fact I *want* to talk to him, makes me realize just how pitiful I am.

I want to ask him his name. I want to know if he has parents, siblings or friends. I wanted to know how many women he had taken and tied to his bed post. I want to know what he intends on doing with me.

Don't be stupid, Scarlett.

I know exactly what he's going to do with me. He's going to kill me when all of this ends; whatever *this* is, exactly, I'm not sure. Everything ends—and for me, it always seems to end with a fucking bang.

I cry into my tied wrists. "Daddy." His name tumbles from my mouth and it gives me permission to break. I break, and it's like all the memories tumble onto the floor. Each one as painful as the last.

A small version of me is sitting on the back door steps, having a cup of tea with him. He seemed so large, and when he looked down at me and smiled, I knew nothing and no one could hurt me, because I had him.

Just how fucking stupid am I?

His laughter haunts me now, as he looks at me with some ice cream on his nose. I'm laughing at him as I eat my own, thinking how silly he is. He never cleaned it off, it just melted from his face. I laugh through my tears as I remember our bath time dance. Shuffling our bums at the full-length mirror that hung on the back door of his wardrobe.

His gray face, that wasn't him. I swore to everyone that they had made a mistake. That man in the wooden box, wasn't my father. My father was a giant, with large hands and a crooked smile. Not the small and old man who lay in the coffin with sunken cheeks. I refused their sympathy. If I did, then he wouldn't be dead. I smiled at them because I knew something they didn't; I knew he would never leave me. He wouldn't. Nope. Not him. I was his princess. I was his everything.

It's too much and I scream into my wrists. I want my necklace, it has kept me safe. It's kept all this pain in. I don't want to exist in this place without him.

I cry until there is nothing left in me to give to this horrible world. I lay my head on my wrists and close my eyes and start to sing. It was a part of me that took me to my happy place. I sang on the streets when I needed money. Recently, with all the rain, there weren't many people around. But, when the sun was out, I often made enough to stay in a cheap hotel.

I sing myself nearly asleep. A noise has me freezing. I open my eyes expecting to see him, but I'm still alone. I listen carefully but I don't hear anything else.

I need to get out of here. I need to get away from him before he kills me. I work the knots on the tie with my teeth. It takes a while and my face is sweaty but I manage to get free. My wrists are red and raw from all the pulling and I rub them as I remove the ties. I don't feel as afraid as I was before. I creep to the bedroom door. The smell of him is all around me, but I know it's coming from his clothes. I try not to think that it's his clothes that are on my body. Opening the door I peek out into the hallway. It's empty as I race down it. I stop at the gym and close my eyes as I try to open the door. It's locked. I glance back up towards the kitchen area. I can hear him shuffling around up there. My feet move quickly across the floor. I enter a room I haven't been in before. It's a small seating area that has a bookcase to the left of the couch and a TV to the right. I'm glancing around the space for something, anything that can help me learn something about him. But there isn't a picture or ornament. Nothing. Even the dark leather couch is empty of cushions. I move to the bookcase and pick up the first book. I'd laugh, but I need to be quiet. It's not even real. I open the storage unit, it's empty inside. Fake books. Christ.

I spend the next few more moments searching the small room but there is nothing. Leaving, I keep close to the wall. I don't hear him in the kitchen anymore. My heart starts to race and I duck into the bathroom. Closing the door carefully, I check the tank and remove the razor.

I need to get the small razors out of the plastic without cutting myself. I place it on the floor to stand on it but I remember I have no shoes on.

"Do you need any help?" I spin and clutch my chest to stop my heart from leaping from me.

He walks over to me, his gaze jumping from my wrists, to my eyes and back down to the razor on the floor that he picks up. "What were you thinking of doing? Cutting my throat while I slept?"

Maybe.

I don't answer him, but look away from his dark eyes. I hate how attracted I am to him. I hate that he has even more control over me than he realizes. But he actually had realized it when my body had responded to his so easily. My face burns again as I think of that. His large hand cups my chin and I hate the softness of his hand. He holds up the razor blade in his other hand. "Were you going to hurt yourself?"

His brows draw down and I can't answer him.

Maybe.

"This is the part where you answer me." His fingers tighten on my chin and a part of me leans into the pain. I can understand it. I can't understand the kindness. *It's a trap*, my mind screams.

"Yes."

His grin is quick. "Yes, to what?" He releases my face and I choose not to answer.

"It doesn't matter. Now I have it." He doesn't say anything about me being out of my binds. Maybe he didn't tie them tightly so I could escape.

I want to scream at him and tell him he's a sick fuck. His combat boots stop at the threshold, he doesn't look at me as he speaks.

"You know the chances of you dying from cutting your wrists, are minimal. You will bleed if you hit nerves, the pain will be excruciating, but most likely it won't kill you." He glares at me over his shoulder. "You'll just make a fucking mess. So don't you dare do it."

He's gone out the door and I have no idea where to go from here. I'm not quiet as I leave the bathroom and move down the hallway. I check the bedroom I had been tied in. Beside that is another bathroom that's bare of everything, even a toilet roll. The gym is after that, which is locked. I don't stop at the small sitting room. I'm surprised the gun room is wide open. He has all these guns, so that means, somewhere, he has the bullets. The hope inside me starts to grow and flourish. I'm not giving up. I'm not lying down—even if it kills me. And it most likely will.

CHAPTER NINE

DEAN

Her red puffy eyes keep diverting to me. I've allowed her up to the sitting area. Some old sitcom plays out in front of me.

"Are you hungry?" I ask when the silence drags out between us. For the first time, I'm aware that someone else is in my space, sitting on my couch. Wearing my clothes. Breathing in the same air as me.

"Yes." Her answer is shy and it carries a note that implies she always is.

"Had you really no one?" I can't understand how anyone in this world could move through it with no one. Especially someone like her.

"What?"

"Ending up on the streets, was there really no one else?" I ask.

Her face heats and she buries her chin into her knees. I let it lie as I make her some pasta. I glance at her and she's watching me again. I hide a smile. I want to ask her to sing. I've never heard anything so beautiful, yet so haunting before. Her voice doesn't belong in a place like this. *She* doesn't belong in a place like this.

She doesn't answer me and I try to focus on what I'm doing. Her silence is frustrating. Each time I take a peek at her, she's watching or glancing around the room. It makes me look at the large space. It's bare and impersonal. I've removed the lamp that she used to try to kill me. I also removed all the knives. There isn't much more she can use against me. Yet, that's what it looks like as her gaze scours the area. It's like she's searching for her next weapon. Once again, I think I should just drop her back on the street. She could never bring anyone here, she was out cold when I brought her to my home. I always keep hidden, I would just have to be extra careful for a while. It would stop whoever is blackmailing me, and the blackmailer knows Gage is my brother. The more I think about it, the more uncomfortable I become. They sent a message, but were able to hide their number. The average person on the street doesn't know how to do that. It was someone technical. Someone prepared.

I stir the pasta before turning it down. The boiling water looks like a weapon and I hesitate on leaving the room, but decide I'll just be more careful coming back in.

"I'll be a minute—don't leave the couch."

Kate bobs her head and I can see the lie in her eyes. Irritation rips through me. Her lids flutter closed and I leave before I change my mind and drag her with me. Before stepping into the gun room, I glance back out into the hall. She's quiet. For now.

Closing the door, I get out my phone. When it's powered up, I hate how no messages or missed calls ping. I dial Gage's number.

"Have you heard anything?" I ask the moment he answers. My hand curls and uncurls, wanting to grip something. I have too much tension bouncing around in my body and no way to release it. I think of the Boyne Club. I just might try to go there later.

The Boyne Club would normally ease me, but for the first time the thought of it doesn't. It does the opposite.

"I told you, I'd ring you." Gage's words are clipped and that pisses me off further.

"How do they know you're my brother? How did they get your number?"

"I have a tech guy trying to hack the number, but so far it isn't easy. I don't think it's about the money." Gage sounds like he's stopped walking. "I think it's about you." His voice has lowered.

"Why ask for fifty grand?"

"To lure you out. Think about your profession. You've never messed up before."

I clench my fist again. He is right. Taking Kate is the biggest fuck up in history. It is just a shame that someone was there to witness it. Unless, she was sent up to that roof on purpose. With her wide-eyed innocence, was she sent to trap me with her looks?

"Did you find out anything about the girl?" Gage asks and I hate how useless I feel right now.

"No. She's homeless. She has no one." I speak, but I'm unsure about the words I say.

"Are you sure?" Gage must hear my uncertainty.

"Yeah." I bite out quickly. "Let me know if you hear anything."

I'm ready to hang up when he says my name. "Dean. Be careful."

I want to laugh and say, 'of what? A small female?' but I'm starting to think she's far more dangerous than I could have ever imagined.

"You too." I hang up and turn off the phone before stashing it back in its hiding place. My eyes are drawn to the wall of guns. Some weapons are in the wrong place. She was at my guns again.

I return to an empty sitting room. The smell of burning pasta has me turning off the stove and pushing the pot to the side. My gaze returns to the couch that I told her not to leave. Yet she had defied me, again. My cock hardens with thoughts of punishing her. I keep my steps quiet as I open the first door and peek into the bathroom. It's empty. A noise comes from the small sitting room. I open the door and she's opening and closing all the books that are just for show.

"Looking for something to read?"

The book slips from her hand and drops to the floor. She glances at me over her shoulder before scooping it up. "Yeah."

The lie slips so easily from her lips. She was in here already. Once again, I noticed the books were moved. When you live alone for as long as I have, any subtle change is noticeable.

"They aren't real." I speak as she slides the book back onto the shelf. She hasn't turned around, but I see the rise and fall of her shoulders. She's nervous.

She finally turns around and her face has grown pale. "I was just bored." She shrugs.

"I told you not to leave the couch." I turn on my heel and walk back to the kitchen. She's moving behind me, her bare feet pad loudly on the wooden floor. She quickly returns to the couch, but it doesn't matter. She defied me so easily.

She's dragged her knees up to her chest again, like I've frightened her, not like she was caught snooping. A part of me wants to lock her up so I can think straight. I scrape the pasta out of the pot and try to separate the burnt ones before pouring a white sauce all over them.

"What did you do before you were homeless?"

I can see her pulse flicker in her neck and I wonder what's making her so nervous. I leave the cooking and return to the couch so I can watch her every reaction.

"I worked at a checkout." She holds her chin a little higher.

"You didn't go to college?" I sit down and she watches me carefully.

"No."

Irritation claws at my skin, is she lying to me? Color enters her cheeks and she shifts on the couch. Her hands tighten further around her drawn-up knees.

"Did you make friends at the checkout?"

"I suppose." She stutters.

"You mean you're not sure if you made friends or not?"

"Yes. I made a friend."

"Name?"

She drops her hands and her feet touch the floor. "Will you kill her?"

"Did she do something wrong that would warrant me killing her?"

The color drains from Kate's face. "Of course not. Does anyone deserve to die?"

Did the man I shot deserve to die? I have no idea. He was a job. He pissed off rich people. What he did, I had no clue; I don't care.

"Some people do," I finally say.

"Do I deserve to die?" Pain blurs her ocean eyes and I clench my fists. Is she fucking with my head?

"You're a thief. So yes."

She flinches and I don't want to talk to her anymore. I've heard enough of her lies. I scoop the cold pasta into a bowl and put it on the table.

"Eat your food," I say. She doesn't move and I glare at her. I'm in no fucking mood. I can't stop the thought that she is here on purpose.

"I'm not hungry." She tries to make herself look small and innocent on my couch.

I move toward her and she screams and scurries back trying to get away from me, but I tighten my hold around her and drag her to the table. I can feel her tremble as I force her into the chair.

"Eat your fucking food." I push the bowl in front of her and she picks up some pasta with her hand before stuffing it into her mouth.

Fuck's sake.

I walk away and get her a fork. She looks up at me when I slam it down beside her. Her chest rises and falls fast, as she stares up at me with fear in her eyes.

Good.

I take my hand off the fork and shove it towards her. She picks it up and starts eating. I'm aware of how much her hand trembles.

I walk away from her before I either hurt her or play out the thoughts that are racing through my head; I want her under me. I want to sink my cock into her. Her disobedience makes me want her more. She is dangerous.

I should have killed her straight away.

I need to kill her.

CHAPTER TEN

SCARLETT

The pasta lodges in my throat and I start coughing. He's glaring at me like I'm spreading a disease throughout his home. I try to cough quieter but the pasta has really lodged in my throat. His hand comes down heavy on my back and I try to get away from his touch. My vision blurs as I continue to cough, I miscalculate my steps as I get out of the chair and land on the ground. I don't have a moment before I'm dragged to my feet. He continues to hammer on my back. This time I don't pull away because I'm actually choking. A new fear clutches my chest. I could die like this. Could my life end over a piece of cold pasta?

"Get it up!" His roar is a command that the food doesn't listen to.

If I survive this, my back will be bruised. His hand comes down heavily and the pasta finally dislodges itself. The air is thin at first as I try to drag it in, his hands are still on me. I hate how aware I am of him. His smell is recognizable to me and I hate that as well. I'm breathing a bit easier when he lets me go and I miss the warmth of his hands on my back. A crash has me tensing. His back is to me, pasta is splattered on the tiles behind the sink, the bowl that holds my pasta is smashed.

I don't move, I try to breathe as quietly as possible. I'm not quiet enough. His gaze zeroes in on me, I can't decipher what I see in his eyes but it sends a shiver skittering along my skin. I feel it bounce and vibrate deep inside me, it's unsettling. I want to apologize to stop whatever is about to come.

He faces me now and I don't dare move as he takes careful steps towards me. He stops at a drawer and opens it. My heart ping pongs in my chest as he holds up my pendant. My father's gift.

He doesn't look at it, he's too focused on me. "Your name is on the back of this." He shakes the pendant and I want to tell him to be gentle with it, his large hand could snap the fragile silver in a second.

I nod as tears clog my eyes. "Yes, it is."

His nostrils flare and his dark eyes seem to go in and out of focus. I have no idea what internal battle he is fighting.

"You want to know my name?" I ask as my stomach twists. I am willing to give it up, because right now, there is something in his eyes that is telling me if I don't pull him back, something bad might happen.

He blinks at my question and the pendant is dropped back into the drawer.

"No. You can no longer speak, Kate. If you disobey me you'll have no food or clothes."

He slams the drawer and leaves the kitchen. He doesn't go down the hall, instead he goes to the door that leads to the outside world. To freedom.

The door opens and he leaves without a second glance. I cover my mouth with my hands. Something between us has changed. Something in his eyes is different.

I'm moving, not wasting a second. My feet are loud on the wooden floor as I race down to the small sitting room. I push the bookcase aside. I noticed a small hole in the wooden floor when I was searching through the books earlier. The blood in my veins roars as the small hole comes fully into view. I'm on my knees, my finger fits into the hole. Elation pours through me as I pull the floor board up. A red and black small passport book sits in the hidden compartment on the floor. My hand shakes as I pull out the black one. Opening it, a fist curls in my stomach as I meet his brown eyes. He's clean shaven in this image and my stomach tightens further. Wow! He's gorgeous. His lips are set in a serious expression making him look dangerous. He is dangerous. My gaze roams across the passport.

Dean Kelsie. Age 34.

Dean, his name is Dean. I close the passport and open the second one. This one is more recent: same name, a different picture, he's sporting his beard in this one.

I can't stop the pure excitement as my hands curl around a small black box. I open it quickly and it's a gun, with bullets. I quickly stuff everything back in and replace the floorboard before pushing the shelf back in place. My heart rate skyrockets as I leave the room. I want to get the gun and be ready, but I'm trembling. I need to make sure that when I take my shot, I don't miss. I leave and enter the bathroom. Splashing my face with water, I meet the wide eyes of a terrified girl. I want to hug her and tell her it's okay. It's nearly over. That we have been through so much, and we can make it out alive. I must make that promise to myself.

I return to the kitchen and decide to sit back on the couch and wait for Dean to come back. Knowing his name makes this worse. He looks like a Dean. If I survive this, anyone with the name Dean will be someone with dark and dangerous eyes, who's a sniper and kidnaps girls. If I survive this, I will run from every Dean.

I'm cold. I don't know if it's the air or the exhaustion that's pulling at my body. I have no idea if it's day or night. Time is funny down here. My mind starts to wander off and I pull it back. Being alone like this with nothing to do is different for me. After spending so much time on the streets, I was constantly on alert, searching for shelter or food. Singing for money.

Singing—that's my happy place—and instead of going to the darkest corners of my mind, I stay present and start to sing. I sing like my life depends on it, because right now, it feels like it does. I feel the difference in the air a while later. The door opens and it's like fresh air filters in. I shiver and pull my feet off the floor. My song dies in my throat as I wait for my fate.

Dean, it's so weird knowing his name, enters and he won't look at me. Dread curls around my spine. He won't look at me. He's closing the door and moving through the kitchen, fear has me speaking.

"Should I clean up the pasta?" The broken dish still lies in the kitchen sink. The pasta is crusting onto his gray tiles. He looks at the mess before he glares at me and I want to disappear. I don't want his attention. I made a mistake, I shouldn't have spoken. It was a lapse in judgement. He's moving so fast towards me again and I'm shaking my head.

Apologize, Scarlett.

"I told you not to speak." He's close to me now, too close. He is leaning in and I feel blocked. I press my lips firmly together.

"Why aren't you afraid?" His question fans across my face and I hate how aware I am of the closeness of his body, or how his fist is pressed into the couch at the right side of my head. His cologne messes with my logic.

"I am," I whisper, as his eyes dance from my eyes and then to my lips.

"I told you not to speak." This time when he speaks, he sounds tired. Fear shoots through me again. He's withdrawing and I make another bad decision. I move quickly and press my lips against his. His eyes remain open and he doesn't respond to me. I move back and his gaze darts across my face. My heart is ready to come out of my chest as he pushes himself away from me, while staring down at me like he can't figure out what just happened. I'm as stunned as he is.

I'm ready to say sorry again, but I know speaking is a really bad idea.

He's breathing heavy and I can't tell what he's thinking. He could be shocked or disgusted. I don't have a clue.

"Get up." I'm on my feet. He doesn't say anything else as he stares at me. I hate how his shoulders rise and fall in quick succession. My vision blurs and he turns away from me. I don't move as he leaves the living space. I stand still as I hear him making noises. One sound registers with me. It's a click-a-click like I made with his guns earlier. My vision swims and I hold still as he returns to the room holding a gun. He pulls the chamber back, he won't meet my eye as he keeps it hanging at his side.

"Walk."

He motions towards the door with the gun. I take a step and pause as I hang my head, a lump in my throat is choking me and I swallow around it.

"Please." My lip trembles and I suck it in between my teeth. When Dean looks at me, his eyes are inky black with no compassion. He points at the door again with the gun. My stomach lurches as I walk.

Outside, the breeze races across my face, whipping my hair into the air as it carries it in all directions. My feet sink into long grass that's still damp from the recent rainfall. Fields and trees, that's all I see as I spin three hundred and sixty degrees. When I stop, I am looking at a large figure all dressed in black. The gun is menacing, but it's his eyes. They are so devoid of life. He's going to kill me. He's brought me out here to shoot me. A calm settles across my shoulders and melts into my bones. I don't look away from him as he raises the gun, there is a moment the walls start to close in and panic consumes me in one huge rush.

Run!

"Don't move." His warning has my bare feet sinking deeper into the grass. I'm shaking my head trying to think of what I did that prompted him to kill me. My mind is a jumble that makes no sense. The last thing I can think of is that I kissed him. Was it that? Does it matter? I've known this is how it'll end.

Tears burn my eyes, and I'm so tired. "Can you put my pendant on?" I ask. My voice is small and I wonder if he heard me. I need my daddy right now.

"Turn around."

I try to plead with him as he raises the gun. My chin tucks into my chest and I hunch my shoulders forward and turn around. The wind continues to whip my hair around and I want to grab it and pull it back down but I don't dare move.

I don't want to die. Not here in a field with Dean. There is so much I still want to do. I want to create a life, I want to watch my hair change from brown to gray.

A sob seeps from my trembling lips. I had so many places I wanted to see. I wanted to stand on the Great Wall of China, or visit the Pyramids. I have too much in me and I have things I've never said out loud. Right now, they bubble up my throat as I stand hunched waiting for the bullet.

"I was abused!" I shout to the wind. The air is thin and my chest tightens. I open my eyes and catch glimpses of the trees through strands of brown hair. "My uncle abused me for years."

There is something freeing in saying it. "I never told anyone. I kept it hidden."

Tears trickle down my face. "I left my auntie's home when she died. I didn't want to be abused anymore." Maybe this is the only way the abuse will ever truly stop. Maybe it'll take me being six feet under. I want to scream at God for the injustice that seems to be my life. But deep down, I know it's my fault.

"I never said no. I never told him to stop. I never said no." Tears fall faster, yet something more blossoms in my chest. It's a secret that weighs too heavily on my soul, a secret that is eating me inside out.

"I'm not ready to die, Dean!" I roar. I need to heal, I need to live. I need to live in a world where I don't hurt. It exists. I know it does.

"Please, Dean."

The ground to my left explodes twice, sending clay into the air. I cower and cover my head from the bang of the gun that erupts twice. There is a moment where it's like the world is suspended before it crashes.

My scalp burns and I'm twirling, the world rotates as Dean's hand tightens on my hair. He turns me, making me look at him. I recoil from his anger but I can't get far from his painfully tight fingers.

His roar is fueled with rage that has the child in me running. I shrivel as he roars again—this time into my face, before releasing me abruptly. I tumble to the ground. The gun is still in his hand as he walks away from me.

All I can think of is that, I'm. Still. Alive. My hand slides across Dean's top that has no holes in it. Tears continue to race down my face and I'm watching him pace back and forth across from me. He's fighting some internal battle that I don't want to be on the losing side of.

The trees aren't far away, they are so green, they are hope. They are a new start and I'm up running, tearing through the grass under my feet. I make it into the trees; the branches tear at me like clawed hands as I run blindly. The bang of a gun has me hitting the ground hard.

I roll onto my back. His military boot lands on my chest and keeps me down. I can't breathe as I try to get him off me. The weight is gone and he drags me to my feet. I have to lean back to see his angry eyes. I'm waiting for him to drag me back to the field or the house but he doesn't. Instead he buries his head in my neck and I'm sure he's sniffing me.

My hands reach up to his shoulders. He doesn't stop the contact and I'm all messed up but right now I need some form of a human touch. Even if it's rough, it means I'm alive. I'm here.

I move closer to him and he doesn't stop me as I lean my head against his chest and listen to his heart crash around inside him.

We stay in this oddness for a while. My aching feet and the cold of the evening have me leaning out. He doesn't let me go far as his hand moves down to my arm, he directs me back to the house. I feel each bite of the forest floor.

Dean stops walking and before I can ask why, he scoops me up into his arms without saying a word. I can't look away from him but his eyes are focused on the house. He doesn't look at me once as he carries me back. When we pass the spot where I had thought I would die, I keep looking at it over his shoulder.

The barren room we step into has a doorway that leads to his domain. My fingers tighten around his neck, and it's the first time he looks at me. This time, I swear, I can see gold swirl in his dark eyes.

"Close your eyes." He speaks so gently but I do as he asks. I don't know why. I think he might kiss me, and since I'm alive, I think I'd like that.

I hear the punch of the buttons and realize that he is putting in the code.

I'm waiting for him to move, or to tell me to open my eyes, but neither happens. I tighten my hold on his neck. Colors burst behind my lids and I follow the red dots as my heart slowly picks up. I want to open my eyes but worry has me keeping them closed. Time ticks away and I finally give in and open them slowly. My heart stills when my eyes clash with his, he's watching me. He's looking at me.

He sees me.

I feel more naked than I did without clothes. But I won't look away. I want to say something to end this interrogation on my heart.

No, not my heart. It's my soul that I have bared to him. My nose and throat burn with a rush of pain that comes from deep inside me. My grief leaks over and all I can think is I am in the arms of a monster; yet, right now, he is all I have. He might be all I ever have. I might not leave this place.

He nods like we have established something. I have no idea what it is, but he walks into the bunker with me firmly in his arms.

CHAPTER ELEVEN

DEAN

I've killed more people than I care to admit. I've never seen them as people, they have always been a target, a means to an end. But with Kate, I couldn't pull the trigger. I think I knew that the moment I told her to come outside. The moment she looked around her like it was the last time she'd see the sky or the trees, but when she turned around and faced away from me, her small body had curled in on itself and I knew I couldn't pull the fucking trigger.

I was abused. When the words about her abuse started to leave her lips, I wanted to kill like I was a man fighting for air. Emptying the gun into the ground did nothing for me. I wanted her to stop, I didn't want to hear her confession about blaming herself. All I wanted was to find her uncle and chop his fucking head off. A bullet would be too good for him.

She's still in my arms, I know she's terrified. I don't fucking blame her but right now I need to hold her. I want her to find comfort in me. I can sense her battle and I pull her closer as I sit down on the couch. Blood drips from her feet, but those cuts will heal, the damage inside her is so much worse. I want to tell her it wasn't her fault, but I can't speak right now without wanting to roar. So I continue to hold her. She's so small in my arms and I'm aware of where my hands touch. Her back heaves against my arms. I like her warm breath on my chest. My lips press against her head, she stiffens in my arms. I have so many questions I want to ask, but so many I don't want the answers to. What age was she when he first put his hands on her? Where the fuck was her father or auntie? Why does she blame herself?

"Dean." My name. She says it again. She had said it outside and I was so sure I had misheard her, how does she know my name? I don't want her to be involved with the blackmailer but it is looking that way. She must have set me up. Anger laces my hands tighter on her and I feel her panic as she starts to squirm.

Let her go.

I release her quickly and grab her before she tumbles to the ground. She has lines of tiredness under her eyes.

"I need to use the bathroom."

I nod and she slides off the couch. Small droplets of blood drip from her feet. I need to bandage them up for her. I focus on the wall in front of me as she closes the bathroom door.

I imagine her uncle: I see him walking down a sidewalk, I place a newspaper under his arm. He's wearing heavy brown boots and a matching belt. He's sure of himself, comfortable in his own skin. He thinks he's

71

someone special. I'm ready to take my shot. I'm always so still, but now I make a sound because I want the fucker to see it coming, his blue eyes look up at mine and they widen, color drains from his face and I pull the trigger. The bullet tears through his forehead, ripping skin and smashing bone. It enters his brain, dragging everything with it until it reaches the back of his skull and explodes against the white—wash wall of the coffee shop behind him. He tumbles to the ground with that same expression of shock and I lie still and watch the pool of blood grow wider. It's satisfying for a second, but he won't die that way. It has to be so much fucking worse.

I glance towards the hall. I don't hear any noise and that has me moving. The water is running when I enter the bathroom. She's in the shower, sitting on the floor fully clothed. I don't ask her what she's doing, she's a fucking mess. Lowering myself to the floor, I sit across from the shower where I can see her. She doesn't look up at me. The blood from her feet dilutes as it washes down the drain. I've seen so much blood, I've spilt so much blood and I've never blinked before. Watching Kate's blood swirl down the drain has the oddest effect on me. It makes the substance have value, it's like her body is crying. She has her head bent, I'm tempted to crawl into the space and lift her chin up. I want to see those ocean eyes, even swimming in pain they are still beautiful. Her shoulders shake as she cries, and I focus on the ceiling and smile as I picture cutting her uncle up. I decide that the auntie is still alive and I make the uncle watch me butcher her first before I kill him. It passes the time blissfully for me.

She's shivering and I think it's shock. Shock from what she admitted, shock from almost dying. Guilt churns in my stomach and I stand up. She doesn't move as I step in and turn off the water. Kneeling down, my boots splash in pockets of water.

"Kate," I say her name and she doesn't respond. It reminds me it's not her name.

I touch her arm gently and her head snaps up to me, her eyes are haunted and I wonder what's playing on the big screen for her. I wish I could watch, I wish I could see what the motherfucker looks like. I help her to her feet. She doesn't object as I pull the wet jumper over her head. Her large breasts bounce free and I can't stop the blood that rushes to my cock. I pull down the sweat pants; leaning down, she holds onto my shoulders. She steps out of them. She's so perfect. Her eyes slowly move up to mine and it takes everything in me not to grab her and take her against the wall. I occupy my mind with getting her a towel for her body. My cock grows harder as I wrap the towel around her.

"I need to look at your feet."

She nods as she pulls the towel from her shoulders and wraps it under her arms, tucking it in so it stays in place. I grab her another towel for her hair and she wraps it up herself. Getting the first aid kit, she hobbles back out to the couch. Her feet are so small in my hands, and I like kneeling down on the floor so I can look up at her. Right now, I look up to find her watching me. A small amount of color has entered her cheeks.

My cock hardens further when I think about all that bare flesh under the towel. She sucks in her bottom lip, I don't think she's aware she's doing it, but I have to look away.

Her feet aren't too bad. It's more scrapes than anything else. None of them have gone too deep. I clean them gently with disinfectant wipes. She hisses and I pause, hating that I hurt her. When she settles, I rub a small amount of cream onto both her feet.

"You'll have to lie here for a while until it dries."

She nods her head. "Thank you."

Her gratitude makes me feel like a shitty human being, so I don't respond. I repack the first aid kit and go get her clean clothes. I'm tempted not to give her clothes; I want to go back to her walking around naked. I find a blue t-shirt that's close to her eye color and fresh sweatpants. I also grab a pair of socks for her feet. She's still lying on the couch when I return. I was half expecting her to be gone.

She follows my movements as I place the clothes on the opposite couch. She's lying with her hands joined on her abdomen. The lines under her eyes are stark. She needs rest. I sit down on the couch beside her clothes. She closes her eyes as she looks away from me. A solitary tear flows down the side of her face. I watch it darken the black leather under her.

"I heard you sing."

She sniffles and nods but doesn't open her eyes. "I like singing."

"Why don't you sing?" I ask. She doesn't respond.

I sit back on the couch and just watch her lie there. No more liquid leaks from her eyes but when she opens her mouth and starts to sing, somehow it's worse.

Her voice shakes, and the haunting melody has my heart picking up pace as she sings about a hanging man having no one to visit his grave. It's eerie and sad but from her mouth, it's beautiful.

74

CHAPTER TWELVE

SCARLETT

I wake and my confused mind can't make anything out. The bed under me is soft, the body beside me is warm. My heart kicks up before my eyes spring open. He's an inch from my face. Dean's asleep on his side facing me. I try to control my breathing as it fans across his face but he's so close. I roll quickly onto my back and stare at the ceiling as I try to calm my racing heart and mind. I squeeze my eyes tightly as I remember the ground exploding beside me as Dean emptied his gun into the grass, instead of my body. I open my eyes and glance at him now, my heart flutters before it gallops.

"How did you sleep?" His gaze roams my face and I don't know what to make of him. My hands tighten around the towel that still covers my body.

I must have fallen asleep on the couch. I don't remember him lifting me. He's still in his dark clothes from yesterday but he looks fresh, like he had a solid night sleep. I'm all too aware of how bad I must look.

"I slept." I frown as I look away from his prodding eyes. I want to ask him why he didn't kill me. I want to ask what happens now, but I'm not naïve. I know him letting me go isn't going to happen. I could promise not to tell anyone.

I look at him again and he's still watching me, even if I was in my prime health he wouldn't be good for my heart.

His bottom lip is bigger than his top and I find my eyes constantly drifting to it. My cheeks heat as I remember singing him a song my father used to sing to me.

Anger laces with everything in my body as I think of my father's pendant that he won't return. That was always my armor. I would touch it and it would give me strength. No wonder I'm breaking apart without it.

"Why didn't you kill me?" My question comes out louder than I intended. Dean doesn't so much as blink as he stares down at me.

"I have my reasons." His words are slow and controlled, not giving anything away.

"If those reasons change?" I question as my heart picks up a fast pace.

"Don't give me a reason to change them."

I frown, and my confusion deepens as he moves quickly. His lips land on mine and I am already used to the feel of them. My bones want to sigh and I have a want to lean into him and accept his touch. His hand feels heavy on my hip bone, the heat travels right through the towel and I hate the wetness that starts to pool between my legs. I tighten my thighs and he leans out of the one-sided kiss. His chest moves fast and the darkness in his eyes has every logical thought in my mind scattering.

"Don't hurt me," I say, as fear skitters quickly across my skin.

A yelp tumbles from my lips as he drags me under him and pins my hands above my head.

"Have I hurt you?"

I bite the inside of my jaw to keep the panic that claws inside me at bay.

He shakes me. "Have I hurt you?!" His roar has me closing my eyes.

"Do you want me to hurt you?"

My eyes spring open and I'm shaking my head. He joins my hands together using only one of his free hands. He drags the towel aside and I'm ashamed when his fingers plunge easily inside me. I bite down on the groan that wants to fall from my lips, his hard cock is pressed against me and I hate the want I feel. I want him inside me. A part of me wants to give in and see what it would feel like to have Dean. His fingers leave me and he dances them across my clit, I arch as all my nerves buzz and this time I can't keep the moan at bay.

Everything in me freezes as Dean releases me and gets off the bed. I'm confused until he pulls the black t-shirt over his head. My heart is frozen in my chest with fear and want. His muscles bunch and flex as he drops the black t-shirt to the ground. His wide shoulders move up and down as he walks back to the end of the bed.

I swallow around the lump that's formed in my throat as he unbuckles his belt. "How do you know my name?"

He pops open the button of his trousers before pushing them down.

I'm ready to get off the bed, his eyes warn me not to move as he climbs on the bed in just his boxers. His large hands grip the towel and I shake my head as he pulls it from around my body, the material burns my skin before the cool air kisses my flesh.

His hands run along my legs that I keep tightly shut. My hands try to cover my large breasts. I try not to look at the huge bulge in his boxers, it's exciting and terrifying.

I can't tell him how I know his name. "I heard you say it."

His grin has no humor and it sends a shiver racing across my bare flesh.

He forces my legs apart. "You are not a good liar."

"Don't," I whisper, but I'm not sure I even mean it. He's there and I'm getting wetter.

"I'm only asking you a question, Kate."

Kate. I hang onto that. I take a calming breath. *You are not Scarlett. You are Kate.*

You are Kate.

You are Kate.

"I heard you say it," I speak louder and look at him. Maybe Kate had heard him say it.

I see the indecision in his eyes. I arch my back as he dips his fingers inside me again. His lips touch my neck.

"That sounded a bit more truthful. But not quite." He pushes another finger in and all I can think of is how badly Kate wants his cock.

I move my face so my lips line up with his. I see the confusion and I kiss him; he freezes again and doesn't return it, instead he pushes another finger inside me and it's too much. I want to tell him to remove one when his head moves and his mouth consumes one of my nipples, he bites it and I cry out. I'm torn between wanting this to end and getting lost in it.

It's wrong. My mind screams.

His teeth clamp harder and the pain is too much, I'm ready to push him off when he releases me, his eyes swirl as he removes his hand from my pussy. He leans out again as he stares down at me.

"How do you know my name?" He asks while dragging his boxers down his legs, his cock springs free and I can't look away.

"I heard you say it." I repeat as he kicks off his boxers, he separates my legs and they ache at how far they are stretched.

"You keep lying to me, Kate."

He moves up my body, his cock sitting at my entrance. He's so much bigger than I am. I should be terrified, but the excitement that bubbles through me has me leaning up and pressing my lips against his again.

Once again he doesn't return it or close his eyes. "I'm going to bury my cock inside you and fuck you so hard until you tell me how you know my name."

Fear starts to dry me up and the deadly situation I'm in has me starting to drown in fear.

"I heard you say it!" I shout before adding. "My name is Kate." I need to clarify who I am in all this.

His cock slams inside me and there is nothing nice about the pain that shoots through me. I'm stunned for a moment before he slides back out of me. I don't get a moment before he slams his cock back in with a brutality that has my body rejecting him.

His mouth consumes my nipple again—as his hands restrain me—and I feel the buds of ecstasy start to rise as he slams his body into me. His teeth graze my nipple and I cry out from the mixture of pain and pleasure.

My pussy grows wetter and Dean moves faster inside me. His mouth releases my breast. His breath fans across my neck. "How do you know my name?" Each word is delivered with a heavy thrust inside me.

I call out as each one is harsher than the one before. I'm a bundle of nerve endings and pain.

I cry out as he sinks his teeth into my shoulder without slowing his thrusts. Tears seep from my eyes with the pain. I want to tell him to stop but I can't as that ecstasy continues to blossom. His pace quickens inside me as his teeth leave my flesh. His hands tighten around my wrists painfully.

"Answer me."

Angry, dark eyes bore into me and when his lips slam against mine, I meet his with my own frantic need that fills each part of me. I have no idea what I'm searching for but I'm rocketing through everything as his tongue enters my mouth. His thrusts are brutal against my pussy. The sting from his skin connecting with mine has me curling my nails into my palms.

His teeth nip my lip and I try to pull away but I'm not quick enough before he bites the sensitive skin. I don't pull as the pain increases along with his pounding. My nails sink further into my palms until a warm liquid erupts from the abuse on my skin. A metallic taste fills my mouth and he releases my lip and hands, and moves back stretching me even further as he loses himself in a frenzy, and I'm right there with him as he pours his seed inside me. I scream out, letting all my control slip and just give in to this madness.

I can't breathe as I come down off the high and Dean takes his huge cock out of me. I'm aching everywhere. I don't even know where to start. I swallow a mouth full of blood, and some part of me, maybe the part that is Scarlett, feels an overwhelming sense of shame. I try to quiet the voice, telling it that it wasn't Scarlett that did this thing. It was Kate.

Dean is still leaning between my legs, sweat coats his chest and he's just watching me as I fight for air and some sanity in all this.

CHAPTER THIRTEEN

DEAN

I can't take my eyes off the blood that mars her perfect plump lips. Her skin is raw and red from where I bit her shoulder and breasts. My eyes trail down as my seed seeps out of her tight pussy. Her thighs are red too, but it's her hands that are still above her head and open, it's the small pool of blood that sits in them that does something to me. It stirs a primal need to protect her. It is fucking laughable that I would feel like that about her.

Her eyes are wild and she reminds me of a trapped animal. My body is still humming from the release. It was so fucking good and I want her again. She still gasps for air and I can't look away from her. I don't move but keep eye contact as she stumbles around whatever the fuck is going on in her pretty head. I want to see what she sees. I want to know what she's thinking.

"How do you know my name?" I sound breathless. My question is so fucking stupid. I know how she figured it out and it has allowed me to breathe. She discovered the safe in the sitting room. She hadn't put the shelf back straight. I've removed the bullets from the gun. I'm curious to see if she will still get it, and if she does, will she pull the trigger?

"I heard you say it."

I grin, and her lies are enough for some of my guilt to dissolve. I've been rough with her. I want her to trust me enough to tell me that she had found my safe. But I have no right to demand her trust—that was shattered a long time ago. Guilt tightens inside me again and I don't want to face it. I slide off the bed and go to the bathroom across from my bedroom. Taking out a face cloth, I run it under the warm tap before grabbing a towel.

She hasn't moved an inch. Her gaze bounces around the ceiling like it might answer questions that I want to know. She's confusing as fuck. She wants me—but she also looks at me like I repulse her.

Her eyes flick to me as I crawl back up on the bed, she tracks my movements and I move back in-between her legs as my cock grows hard again but I won't take her. She needs someone to mind her, even if it's only for a moment.

"Give me your hands." I hold out one hand and am surprised when she obeys me and places her small hand in mine. She doesn't flinch or hiss as I clean the blood away. The half-moons are visible when I brush away all the blood. I hate that she inflicted that upon herself. I wonder if she finds pleasure in hurting herself? It makes me think of the razor blade she was hiding in the bathroom. I look at her again to find her watching me. She's so beautiful.

Hauntingly beautiful.

She's the type of girl that you would never really understand or figure out. She's a minefield that I don't mind crossing.

"Do you play the piano?" I ask, as I continue to clean her hand and try to distract myself from the thoughts that swirl around my head. She doesn't pull away from me like I expect.

"No, but I always wanted to."

I glance at her and her green eyes have lost the wild look they had held only a few moments ago. Now they are filled with regret.

"Give me your other hand." She gives it to me and I watch her blood turn the white face cloth red in places. Once again she doesn't pull away or hiss as I clean her hands.

"You have piano fingers," I say, as I trail two of my fingers down the length of hers. She needs to learn to play the piano. I can only imagine her playing it while singing.

Priceless.

"Do you play an instrument?"

I grin at her. "I only play with guns."

She doesn't smile at my joke, but it's not really a joke. My job is my hobby. I love what I do. I frown, not liking where my mind is going. I like taking lives, but not hers. I won't take hers. What the fuck is wrong with me? I tell myself it's because I wasn't paid to kill her, but deep down I know if someone did, I would turn it down.

"I like to fish," I say, trying to take the fear out of her eyes. When I was a kid, I used to fish with my father but we never bonded. He wasn't an asshole, but I spent too much time wanting to push him into the river so I could spark up the joint that was crushed in my back pocket.

"Do you have siblings?"

"A brother. I think he'd like you," I say the words and regret them instantly as she frowns at me before cutting me off.

"But you knew that already." I fire out as I release her hand. She's staring at me again. I'm watching and looking for the tells of any lies.

"That you have a brother?"

"Yes." I lean out more and touch her thigh with the cloth. She jerks and I take a quick look at her as I run the cloth along her pussy cleaning up my seed. Her eyes swirl and I see the need in them. The same need grows in me.

"I didn't know you have a brother." Her words are breathy as she speaks and I continue to run the cloth along her pussy. I press it against her clit and she reacts, arching her back up to meet the piece of fabric.

"What's your biggest fear?"

She seems to be rousing out of her lust and she thinks about what I'm asking. I run the cloth along her clit again before dipping a finger inside her.

"Oh, God!" She moans to the ceiling.

"God?" I ask, knowing that's not what she meant.

"No." Her breathy word has me pushing in a second finger and throwing the cloth aside. Taking my cock in my hand, I give it a stroke. Her eyes focus on my shaft and she bites her lips as I push my fingers into her as far as they will go. I give my cock a few more jerks before I speed up my strokes.

"Touch yourself." I tell her, removing my wet fingers from her pussy. She slides her hand down and I watch her fingers work quickly on her clit.

Fuck me! My body roars and I want to pound into her but I also want to watch her touch herself.

"Make yourself cum for me."

She rotates her fingers around her clit and I move closer pulling my cock harder. Some of my pre-cum slips out of the fat head of my cock and slides along the side of it. She groans, moving her long fingers faster and I love the liquid I see coming out of her pussy as she groans out loud. My own jerks grow faster and I feel the cum before I splash her leg with my seed. I give my cock a few final jerks until my release is finished. It's not enough, and I know that's not good, that I can't feel satisfied without her.

She's staring at me again and her eyes don't look so haunted. But she does look confused.

"What's your biggest fear?" I ask again because I want to know. I want to know everything about her.

"Getting attached to someone." The words leave her lips that still have blood on them. I reach for the cloth and clean up her leg.

"That's your fear?" I hate that we have the same fear. My gaze flickers to hers and I pause in cleaning her leg. Her eyes swim with tears. Tears that I don't want her to spill. I have no idea what has brought this on.

"What about you?" She asks while she blinks and I expect tears to fall but they don't.

"Rats." I lie easily as I clean my cum off her leg. I don't know if she's fucking with my head by making me want her in more ways than one. I get off the bed and dump the cloth into the thrash before I start to get dressed. She doesn't move and each time I look at her she's lying in the same position. I pause with a weird need of wanting to know what is going through her mind.

"What are you thinking?" I take a step back to the bed but don't get up on it.

She's staring at me. "Nothing."

She shuts down and I'm happy to leave it at that. The more I'm around her, the more I want to be around her. This isn't good. Especially since she is my prisoner and she should be dead. I have no idea where we go from here.

I pull on a clean pair of boxers and put my trousers back on. I get her clothes that I had gotten for her yesterday and lay them on the bed beside her.

I pull on my top and don't say anything as I leave her alone in the room. Too fucking much swirls in my mind, and most of it, I don't want to acknowledge.

CHAPTER
FOURTEEN

SCARLETT

I ache everywhere. I haven't moved since he left the room. A giggle dribbles from my lips. He is afraid of rats. If I could only get my hands on some rats, I could put them in his bed. I roll onto my side and draw my legs up to my chest as my vision blurs. Heartburn causes saliva to pool in my mouth; I've been suffering with heartburn since living on the streets. I tighten my eyes and my tears spill.

There is something terrifying about the softness of the bed under me, it's a reminder of where I used to lie. The fear that used to tighten itself around me when I heard the third from the top step creak late at night.

I knew this was it. I knew I couldn't stop it as my uncle pushed open the bedroom door that he refused to let me lock. I'm far too old now to lie here any longer like this; yet, it's like I've trained my body to do so. *Stay still and it won't be real.* That's what I had told myself. Inside my head, I would crawl to the darkness that waited for me as the bed took his weight. I withered as his hand groped me. The smell of alcohol on his breath sent my heart racing, yet I knew my breathing needed to remain the same. I needed to remain asleep. He's jerking behind me as he touches me and I bite my jaw. I have so many scars inside my mouth from years of biting it to keep the screams in. The screams for it to stop, yet if I spoke, it would be real. It can't be real. I'm not the type of girl who gets abused. That happens to someone in another country, not me.

I drag my knees up higher and sink my teeth into my kneecap which has small white scars from me doing this often. I'm laughing and crying, because I just had sex with my kidnapper.

"Are you okay?"

As I jerk up, my eyes land on Dean who watches me.

No. I'm not okay.

The flash of the silver gun in the black box springs to mind. My stomach twists as I look into dark eyes. It is the only way I can get out of here. I don't want him to see what I'm thinking. My stomach quivers with a sickness at the thoughts that race through my mind. He had so easily taken me outside and put that gun to my head. I know he didn't killed me, but he thought about it. What would it take for him to pull the trigger next time? If I disobey him? If I say something that doesn't like?

"Are you hungry?"

I'm always hungry. The words seep right back into my fragile mind. Fear takes root for so many different reasons.

His eyes drift to my lips and my tongue flicks out. As I lick them, I can taste blood that has seeped from the inside of my mouth. The beat of my heart grows faster and louder as he continues to stare at my mouth.

"No." It is a lie. But I don't think I could honestly keep anything down right now.

He shifts closer and my delicate heart can't take much more of him. I won't be able to keep myself together and I know there is something wrong with me. "Can I get dressed, please?"

My fingers tighten around the quilt under me as something flashes in his eyes and I fear I've pissed him off.

"Why were you laughing?"

I grin, but I don't know why. This can't get much worse. Or maybe it could. Maybe I could end up wanting to stay here with him. The thought has my heart hammering as he waits for me to answer.

"Why am I here?" I fire back. Am I trying to provoke him?

His gaze pins me to the spot before he turns on his heel and leaves the room.

I get out of the bed and grab the blue t-shirt and sweatpants along with the socks that he had left out for me. My feet complain as I step out onto the floor and race to the bathroom.

The water is warm as it drizzles down my back, but I'm hunched over and can't enjoy the wash. There are too many reminders of my past. The closer I get to Dean, the closer I'm getting to the past. He's making me think, he's making me feel, and it's not fair.

My hands run across my stomach and so do Dean's, his light a fire along my skin; older hands touch me now, and I quickly step away from the water's spray and wipe the water from my eyes. I look around the room as blood pounds in my ears. What is happening to me?

I want to call Dean, I want to see him. I want to know this is real. I push my back against the cold tiles, my heart starts to slow as I press my aching palms against them and I start to sing. I sing low as I try to calm myself. I sing about a dying child and a broken hearted mother. I sing what my father sang. I sing the heartache that smashes into my chest. I don't stop until my head stops spinning and my vision clears. Only then do I get out and start to get dressed. I find it hard to meet my own eyes in the mirror. Rings circle under them and there is a part of me that's ready to lie down and let it be, whatever *it's* meant to be. But I see Scarlett at ten years of age, begging me not to give up on her.

My feet appreciate the cushion from the socks on my soles. They sting as I step out into the hallway. I need to get the gun from the sitting room without him noticing. The hallway is clear and I decide that if I'm really going to do this, I need to keep him busy, I need to be smart about this. I need to get out of here before it completely destroys me. It's taking a toll on my mind.

"Dean." When I say his name, my voice cracks, giving away how nervous I am.

Pull it together.

He seems startled and looks up at me from the counter. I'm not sure what he's looking at, but he stuffs something back under the counter and out of my line of sight.

"I am actually hungry." I try to smile at him but it feels odd on my face, so I stop. He's observing me and I try not to shift under his scrutiny.

"What can I make you?" Guilt churns in my stomach as he smiles at me. I shrug. "I'm easy."

He studies me a bit longer and there is something that flashes across his eyes before he nods.

"Okay."

"I'll go tidy the room." I'm lingering. I don't want to do this, but I remind myself that he backed me into a corner. He kidnapped me. Took my pendant. That's all I need to leave the room.

"Kate."

I look back at him and his pause is long. For one split second, I fear he can read my mind and he knows what I'm about to do. But he smiles.

"What's your favorite sandwich?"

"Banana with just one spoonful of sugar." My throat clogs again as I picture me eating one, sitting on a black and silver chair beside my father's coffin. My legs swung from the height as I ate it while waiting for him to come back for me.

He nods again and I move quickly down the hall before I change my mind. I duck into the sitting room and move the shelf as quietly as I can. Taking out the black box, I rub my hands along my sweatpants drying off some of the sweat before opening the box. The silver gun feels heavy in my hands. My stomach plummets as I see there is only one bullet left. There were more. He must have used them. I don't remember him leaving. I glance up at the door expecting to see him standing there but the doorway is empty. I take the bullet and have to fidget with the gun to get it open but I manage to do it. Sliding in the bullet, I close the gun and twist the revolver. I've never fired a gun, and now—having only one bullet, I can't miss. If I do, he will kill me.

I don't tuck the gun into the waistband of my sweats, fear of shooting myself has me holding it with both hands as I walk back out into the empty hallway. I can hear him moving around in the kitchen and I push the guilt aside. I step into the kitchen area and I hesitate. I don't want to point the gun at him in case it goes off. He turns and he doesn't blink as his eyes trail down to the gun in my hand.

"Give me the code. I just want to leave." My voice trembles.

"No," he says it clearly as he places the banana sandwich on the table.

I raise the gun and hate how I tremble as I point it at him. "This gun is loaded and I will fire." *I don't want to. Please don't make me.*

"You can't leave, Kate."

"Open the fucking door." My fear has my voice growing and he looks nervous now. "I just want to go."

"Where? Where would you go?"

"What kind of question is that? I'm not going to tell you."

He takes a step towards me, like I'm not a threat. "You were on the streets. Would you go back there? Or what? Go to your uncle?"

My hands grow steadier and I'm ready to pull the trigger. "You think this is better?"

"Yes." His answer is quick and honest.

A laugh leaves my lips. "You kidnapped me. I'm being held here against my will."

"Have I hurt you?" He takes another step and I raise the gun higher.

"Just let me go." My stomach twists, where do I go? Back onto the streets he is right. Is this better? No. It has to be my choice and right now, I don't have one.

"Open the door or I will shoot."

"No, you won't." He's nearly right in front of me. If he wants, he can reach out and take the gun. "Just think clearly for a second. You have a roof over your head and food on your table." He holds up his hands like he's really trying to reason with me.

"It's not my choice!" I roar and he takes a step back. "Open the door."

I know he won't. I can see it in his eyes. "If you pull the trigger, you won't get out. You'll die in here. I'm the only one with the code."

I am in a coffin. My stomach quivers and I swallow down the bile that climbs up my throat.

Closing my eyes, something overtakes me and I pull the trigger. The bang sends me spinning, but when I open my eyes, my blood drains down into my feet. I've never seen him so angry. His dark eyes are as black as an abyss that I'm falling into. I keep pulling the trigger and the chamber keeps spinning.

"You pulled the trigger." His words are angry.

Tears trickle from my eyes. I keep pulling the trigger until he rips the gun easily from my hands.

"You knew!" I cry as the gun hits the wall, denting it.

He reaches into his pocket and takes out a handful of bullets.

"Is this what you want?" He moves towards me and I step back. A bullet hits my chest before it bounces on the floor.

"You pulled the trigger!" He roars and I can't get away from his anger as the remaining bullets rain down on me before bouncing onto the wooden floor. My back hits the wall and he towers over me.

"You pulled the trigger!" His roar is filled with hurt and I scream as his fist hits the wall at the side of my head.

His anger is choking me. I knew he would be mad, but this is too much.

"Of course I did. I want out!" I scream at him.

His fist hits the wall again and I want to crawl away from him.

His hands find my hair and he leans into me. His forehead touches mine. I can't breathe with him this close.

"I can't let you leave." His words have me opening my eyes. He releases my hair before pressing his fist against my face and I fear that this is it, he will kill me. His eyes hold nothing but murder in them. He pushes his fist against my cheek and I cry out. He's gone and I slowly slide down the wall as my knees buckle.

CHAPTER FIFTEEN

DEAN

She's still crying and I try to control the need to return to the living space and demand her to tell me why she pulled the trigger. That's exactly what happens when you start to trust someone. They try to fucking kill you.

I get out the phone and switch it on. I have a message from Gage. He wants me to ring him. We have a meeting point. I reach into my safe and take out another loaded gun. If she had found that one, she would have emptied it into me. I grab what I need and pause in the living space. She's still sitting on the floor. Her eyes flick towards me and I hate the hollowness I see in them. I'm ready to leave but I gather up all the bullets off the floor—and the gun. I don't threaten her; I want to, but I think we have moved beyond that point.

I know I need distance from her and her madness. I leave, and once I'm outside, a part of me feels a want. I ignore it as I climb into the truck.

"Did he say where?"

"Can you meet me?" Gage answers my question with one of his own.

"Yeah, I'm leaving now."

He pauses and I'm wondering what else he wants to say. "Okay." He seems to reconsider and ends the call.

I back away from the house and I can't stop the emptiness that seems to stretch the further I get from Kate.

Gage is waiting for me at the entrance to the park. I pull up at the sidewalk and stuff the gun in the glove compartment before getting out. I'm looking around me, wondering if anyone is watching us, ready to pounce. Each building is a possible threat. I've never seen them as a problem, but I've also never been blackmailed before.

I walk up to Gage, who has stopped under a large oak tree. It's drizzling, but that seems to be the weather lately.

"You look like shit." Gage greets me.

My irritation at being here has me scratching my neck. "What did you find out?"

"Thursday, they want to meet you here at noon."

I start to walk. "In two days."

"I reached out to some people and no one seems to know anything, but you know this isn't about fifty grand."

I glance at Gage. He is right. "Yeah, I know. Someone wants me dead."

He nods. "You have two choices. You can either meet this person, or let the girl go and go into hiding."

My stomach twists and I grin. "I'm not letting her go."

Gage's hand tightens around my forearm stopping me. "This isn't a fucking joke."

I pull my arm from his hold. "I fucking know that."

"She could be part of this. Have you thought of that?"

"Kate isn't." I answer far too quickly.

There is an uncomfortable look in Gage's eye. "I want to meet her and question her."

I grin at him. "No. If you have any questions, just ask me." The thought of anyone being around Kate has me wanting to get into my truck and drive home to her.

"You clearly haven't asked her the right questions."

"Say what you really want to say." He thinks she's dead. I can see it in his eyes.

"Is she alive?"

I fucking knew it. "Yes." I grit out through my teeth.

"Have you hurt her?" Now my brother won't look at me. "Just let me meet her and ask a few questions. She might answer them. Women tend to be more comfortable with me."

Gage's voice has softened and I look at him. "I don't fucking know why."

He grins and I find myself grinning back. I can't bring him to Kate, no one knows where I live. I won't reveal that. Taking her out has my stomach twisting.

"I'll meet you back here in a few hours," I say, and surprise flitters through his eyes.

"With her?"

I'm regretting it already but it's Gage. "Yeah."

He nods and I walk back to the truck. I can still just go home and hunker down, but if they have Gage's number, then they know he is my brother and he is in danger too.

I don't return straight to the house. I pull up at a large store that sells a bit of everything. I need to get Kate clothes and some supplies. I spend far too long in the lingerie department. Two women stare at me and I wish I had my gun to wave in their faces so they would run along. I don't get any lingerie. I need to get back. I take jeans and t-shirts, along with boots, socks, and plain underpants to the counter. I also grab a green army jacket for her. With everything loaded into the truck, I drive back.

She's not still sitting on the floor and I drop the bags. "Kate!" I call, not leaving the living space. I remove the gun from the band of my trousers. I'm waiting for her to charge with some sort of weapon, but she softly steps into the living room. Her hair is wet from a recent shower and she's wearing a black t-shirt and sweatpants. Her large ocean eyes widen and I lower the gun.

Her eyes follow my movements until I tuck it back into the band of my trousers.

"We are going out."

She's shaking her head. "I don't want to. I'm fine here."

Me too.

"It's not a choice," I say and point at the bags. "Get dressed."

She takes a step towards the bags but her eyes don't leave me. "Are you going to kill me?"

Her face has paled and everything feels wrong about taking her outside. She's safe in here.

"No."

"Where are we going?" She asks, and I remember she pulled the trigger, and that I'm mad at her for that.

"Get dressed, and stop asking me questions."

She stands taller and I want her to defy me. I want her to give me a reason to put my hands on her. She doesn't; instead she grabs the bags and takes them out of the living space.

I make us both a sandwich. I'm tempted to make her favorite, but she doesn't deserve that right now.

When she returns, she pulls at the tight red t-shirt that's painted to her skin. My cock hardens straight away.

"I made you a sandwich." She sits down in her usual spot and I slide her plate down to her before sitting down with my own. We eat in silence and I can't stop staring at her. I shouldn't take her out. It isn't safe.

Gage is my brother and he won't hurt her, I remind myself.

"Dean." Her voice is low. I hate how nice it is to have my name on her lips. "What's going to happen to me?"

Fear clouds her eyes and I soak it up. "That depends on you."

I finish my sandwich and hate how hers has only one small bite missing.

"Eat," I say, before getting up and pouring out a drink of water. I gulp half the glass down before turning and giving her the other half. I hold the glass so her lips will touch where I drank from, she takes it from me and my trousers tighten further.

"Do you still want to leave?" I ask her as I look down at the crown of her head. She doesn't look up at me. Her hand tightens around the bread and it's squished between her fingers.

"I don't know." She sounds tired.

"Put on your jacket." Her head snaps up to mine and she shakes her head again.

I laugh. "You've been trying to escape since you arrived here, now you get to leave and you don't want to."

She's looking towards the door with a longing in her eyes before glancing back at me. "I don't know what's going to happen out there." She points towards the door and I kneel down so we are eye level.

"I never know what you are going to do in here. You keep trying to kill me."

She swallows and her eyes fill with tears. "You are going to kill me." She's nodding like it's the answer to it all.

"Get your coat on." I rise and she scrapes the chair along the floor. I don't notice how perfectly the coat fits her.

Each step we take up the stairs has me wanting to take her back down. I hate how she looks to the sky when we step outside. I open the passenger door of the truck. "Get in." She turns and stares at me but does as I tell her. Her shoulders fall forward as I close the door. She doesn't speak as we leave the property, she's taking it all in. I shouldn't allow her but it reinforces the knowledge that she can never go. I can never let her leave me. It only takes fifteen minutes to arrive back into the town. I see the recognition in her eyes when we pull up to the park.

"We are so close."

"We are meeting someone who wants to ask you some questions. Answer them and that's it."

"Who? Why?" Her chest rises and falls quickly and I don't like the fear in her. It's not caused by me but her belief that someone else might hurt her. I unclip my seatbelt.

"Listen to me, Kate. No one is going to hurt you. Not when I'm around." I need her to believe me. I'll never let anyone hurt her. She quickly glances out the window before she looks back to me. Her emotions vanish and now it's my turn to feel fear.

"Don't you dare try to run." I warn and lean into her.

"I won't."

I unclip her seatbelt. "Why do you lie so much?" The snap of her seatbelt has her tightening her eyes.

"I don't understand what's happening." She sounds tired again and I hate what I am putting both of us through.

"We'll be home soon." I touch her beautiful face and she moves away from me. Then I remember she pulled the fucking trigger. I get out and walk around to her door. Opening it, she climbs out. I take her hand in mine. It feels so right. She does that thing again as I lock the vehicle: she stares up at the sky like she hasn't seen it before. I lead us to the park.

"Dean." Her voice is small again and I squeeze her hand.

"I know where you live." I glance at her and she doesn't look afraid, she looks resigned. "You're going to kill me, aren't you?"

I look around me and my stomach twists. I can see Gage walking to us in the distance.

"No. But I don't want you to answer any questions without my approval."

"How will I know?" Her eyes follow where I am looking, and I squeeze her hand so she refocuses back on me.

"I'll nod my head. If you say anything else, I won't kill you, Kate. I'll hurt you."

She looks away from me again. I grip her chin and make her look at me. "Do you understand?"

"Yes." Her one word is filled with so much defiance and I can't stop the grin that tugs at my lips.

My grin slips as Gage stares at me, his eyes taking in our joined hands as my other hand holds her chin.

"Hi." His voice rumbles and captures Kate's attention. I don't like it. I don't like it one bit.

CHAPTER SIXTEEN

SCARLETT

My fingers tighten further on Dean's. I don't know this other person and have no idea what he wants. Looking into his face reminds me of Dean's, only Dean's is stronger. They have the same eyes, only Dean's always feels like they are tinged with something indescribable, like madness.

"Hi." His deep voice has me stepping closer to Dean.

I look to Dean and he nods at me.

"Hi," I say back. I could scream or run across the open park. The shop isn't far from here, would someone help me? My focus zones in on a woman running on the other side of the green lawn, if we stand here long enough she will pass and I can scream then. My heart starts to race.

"What's your name?" The stranger asks and I look to Dean, he nods.

"Kate," I answer automatically.

"Do you have family?"

"I already told you she doesn't." Dean speaks up for me but the stranger doesn't take his eyes off me.

"Did he hurt you?" He sounds so sincere; his words are a little rushed.

Dean tugs me away from the stranger.

"Are you fucking serious? You said you had questions." Dean pulls me further behind him and I keep watch on the runner.

"Let her go." The stranger steps closer to us. "You know this is too fucked up."

"That's why you brought me here? To take her?"

"Take her?"

The runner is getting closer and hope blossoms inside me. Dean takes a step towards the stranger. "Yeah, take her. She has nowhere to go. I told you, she's homeless."

I look back to them, hating how they are talking about me. The stranger's eyes meet mine. "Are you homeless?"

I look to Dean, who nods.

"Yes," I answer.

"Someone is blackmailing my brother. They want fifty thousand or they will release the image of you."

"What the fuck, Gage?" Dean releases my hand and pushes his brother. "What are you doing?"

And I'm standing here. I'm free. Gage looks at me, his eyes dart to the runner who's watching me, too. She nods at Gage and her pace quickens. "It's okay." She grabs my arm and I'm moving with her.

"Run!" I'm moving. I'm running away from Dean. There is this tiny part of me that feels a sense of confusion. The blast of a gun has me and the jogger hitting the ground.

"Dean!" Gage shouts.

I look up from the ground to see Dean with the gun trained on Gage as he walks back to me.

"Get up." He holds out his hand and a whimper leaves my lips.

"You can't keep her." Gage moves towards Dean.

"You fucking tried to trick me." The jogger covers her head as the gun is waved at her skull.

"Just let her go and all this ends." Gage begs Dean and he glances at me.

I plead with my eyes for him to let me go but I already know the answer.

"Get into the vehicle." He points at the truck but I don't move.

"Kate!" His raised voice makes me jump.

"That's not my name!" I'm shouting back. It's all I have left—this tiny snippet. Dean's too consumed with getting me back into the truck to care about my name.

"See, she's lying. That's not her name. What else is she lying about? She might be the blackmailer. She might be in on it."

Dean doesn't let me go as Gage helps the jogger up off the ground.

"Dean." Gage shouts again.

I'm forced into the car and watch the world behind the pane of glass. The jogger keeps her eyes on me.

"She knows what I am. She knows where I live. Letting her go isn't an option." Dean's words cause whatever response Gage had to die on his lips. Dean gets in and starts the truck.

I hate how the jogger keeps looking at me. It's like the last time she will ever see me. I blink and tears fall because I think she's right. I don't think Dean will let me walk away. I sit back in the seat as he tears from the town.

My hand touches my bare neck. "I want my pendant back." The words are heavy on my tongue.

"I can't think right now, Kate." Dean rubs his temple.

"I don't care!" I shout.

He looks at me. "Be quiet." His words are so dismissive.

I stare back out the window as the world flashes past us. It's a split second decision. Do I want to die? No. I want something else. Freedom, control, a choice.

I make the choice to reach across and pull the steering wheel from his hand. We hit the ditch hard. His roar is deafening as he tries to control the vehicle and I'm floating, hair covers my face as the world turns upside down. The seatbelt rips against my chest, stealing away all the air from my lungs. I see the ground fast approaching and curl up as best I can but the impact feels like it smashes every bone in my body. I'm suspended in pain as I slam back into the seat and the world shakes for a few seconds.

The blare of a horn has me lifting my chin off my chest. I see trees, lots of trees. I turn to see Dean's head resting on the horn that continues to blare. My hands work quickly at my seatbelt and I manage to get it free. The door is heavy to push open, and I fall out of the vehicle. My hands sink into the damp grass. I try to stand but the world shifts and I land on my hands and knees. I take a few steadying breaths before I start to crawl. The grass grows wetter the further I move. Pain screams in my left ear and I try to rub it with my shoulder. I glance back at the truck. Smoke billows out from under the hood. I pause, imagining it going up in flames with Dean trapped inside.

Scarlett, he took you. I remind myself before I continue to move across the wet ground. It's starting to sink under my hands. I look up to see a huge lake in front of me. It must have overflowed. I look back again and smoke continues to billow from the car.

Standing, I manage to stay up. I sway with dizziness as my conscience becomes too much, and I find myself swaying back to the car. The horn continues to blare. I try to open Dean's door but it's wedged. I have to go around to my side and crawl back in. His seat belt comes loose easily. I push him back and the noise stops. His head is pretty banged up and some part of me doesn't want to leave him.

Tears blur my vision as I crawl out of the car and start to run. I fall, but each time I do, I pick myself back up. I can't be far from a road. I know that we had been on one before we crashed. I see a blue car in the distance.

"Help me!" I start to run towards it. "Help me!"

I hit the ground hard as a branch snags my trousers. I scramble up again. "Help me!" I start to wave at the car. I'm so close. It's right there. I can almost make out the driver. "Help me!" My shouts turn hysterical.

Something hits my back and I'm on the ground again, only this time I can't get up. Dean spins me around and clamps a hand over my mouth. Blood drips from his head onto my cheek as I scream into his hand. He doesn't say anything but keeps me pinned as I squirm and scream under him. The car is gone. It's gone and I'm looking into dark eyes that torture me.

He removes his hand but I don't stop screaming at the top of my lungs. He keeps me pinned as he just watches me, all my pain seems to latch onto my screams and I want him to stop me again because I can't seem to cut the pain off. My roars turn into cries and I hate him. I hate him for making me sit still and sort through my head; it's like I'm touching each memory and somehow he's making me relive the worst part of me.

"I hate you." I tell him and he doesn't blink.

"I hate you!" I shout louder and he doesn't react.

"I hate you! I hate you! I hate you!"

His lips are on mine cutting off my anger. "I hate you." I mumble against his lips as salty liquid flows into my mouth.

"I hate you." My words are dying slowly as my strength dwindles. His kiss is warm and I kiss him back, when his tongue enters my mouth I open wider for him. I need to go somewhere else and I don't want it to be the dark room anymore. I think I'll go wherever Dean wants to take me. I get lost in the kiss and I hate when he breaks it. He pulls me to my feet. He winces before touching his head. His fingers tighten around mine and we are walking across the wet land towards the lake.

"What are you doing?" I ask. I don't want to die. Is he going to drown both of us?

Dean looks back at me before tugging my hand so that I'm right beside him. I scream as the truck behind us explodes and a ball of fire is released into the air.

"Come on." He tugs me harder and I don't want to go into the water. I try to stop but Dean doesn't pause. He pulls me into his arms, scooping me up against his chest, as he steps into what I thought was a lake. It doesn't go past his knees, as he wades through it. I glance over his shoulder at the smoke that billows from his car. Sure enough, that will attract a lot of people. Even the cops. I look forward and the water seems to go on forever.

"I can walk," I say to Dean. He doesn't release me or answer me. The water circles around us and it's like we are walking on water. I look up into Dean's face. His head is bleeding pretty badly. He's losing a lot of color.

Maybe he'll pass out. His dark eyes flicker to me and guilt churns in my stomach. I fear he knows what I'm thinking.

His steps slow down and I don't offer to walk again. I want to wait for him to collapse. The fire ball behind us grows smaller.

"We are nearly there." Dean's words have dread curling in my stomach. Nearly where? He steps out of the water and only then does he put me down. My feet touch dry ground as he takes my hand and we step out into another field and right there, in the middle, is his fucking house. I stop and swallow the saliva that pools in my mouth.

"Kate." He sounds tired but his hand feels strong around my fingers. He tightens it and we start to walk back to the house. Back to my prison. Back to the box that I will die in if anything happens to Dean.

"Your head is bleeding pretty badly," I say, as a new fear of getting stuck in the bunker takes over.

"Are you feeling bad that you hurt me?" he asks as we start up the steps of the house.

No. I'm afraid of being buried alive.

"Yes." I answer.

He stops outside the large silver door and grins at me. "You lie so much, Kate. Now close your eyes."

"No. What's the point?"

He pulls me into his chest. "Close your eyes." His words are whispered, as his gaze flickers to my lips.

"No." I answer again and he tilts his head to the side.

"Kate."

"That's not my name," I tell him before my eyelids flutter closed. I hear the beep of the code as he presses it in. Each number has a different sound. I've heard it before but I just didn't know what I was hearing. I want to open my eyes as my heart sings. His fingers wrap around mine as I'm led back down into the bunker, only this time I have a bit more hope of getting out of here.

CHAPTER SEVENTEEN

DEAN

My head pounds and I can't even consider leaving Kate for a second. I take her hand once we are inside. She doesn't stop me as I lead her to the bathroom.

I need a shower and I don't trust her to be left alone. No doubt she will try to kill me again. I pull off my top and my side aches. I hear her loud intake of breath. Glancing in the mirror, I see my side is black and blue—I don't think anything is broken. I can't bend to take off my boots. Kate watches me struggle but doesn't offer to do anything about it.

"Could you help take off my boots?" I hold on to the wall to steady myself and she doesn't move. I grin. Of course she won't help. I lower myself to the toilet and manage to pull them off.

"Take off your clothes," I say. I don't have the energy to force her and I'm surprised when the green army jacket hits the floor. I remove my boots and manage to pull off my socks. I don't want her to see how bad I am, so I sit back and pretend to take her in as she pulls off the t-shirt. Her breasts bounce free as she observes me.

"I'd let you go if I could." She freezes at my words and I mean them. If I could turn back the time, I'd let her go.

"You're a liar." Her words are quick as she kicks off her own boots.

"Kate," I whisper her name. I'm not lying. I become transfixed as she pulls down her trousers and underpants. I use all my strength to stand and open the belt of my trousers before I push them down.

Kate steps into the shower and starts the water. My boxers pull down over my large erection. It feels too tight. I've wanted her so badly. I would have taken her in the field with all her anger but I didn't want us to get caught.

I step in and her eyes skip to my erection before they travel back up to my eyes. Color tinges her cheeks.

She steps towards me and I can't decipher what I see in her eyes. Pain, anger, lust, a realization? I'm not sure.

"My name is Scarlett. I'm twenty-one years old and I love the color green. Not mint green, or light green." She shakes her head. "I like the green you'd find at the bottom of a blade of grass. The green that no one would ever put on their walls. I like that green. I hate birds and I've always wanted to let off those lanterns in the sky at night time, like they do in China." She steps closer to me and I try to control my beating heart.

"This moment, right now, is my choice. So please, don't take it from me." She leans in and presses her lips against mine. I don't want to kiss her back. I don't want to give her that kind of control over me, yet my lips move

112

under hers and my hands go to her waist. Her flesh is warm under my touch and it doesn't feel right to let her lead. Her kisses are soft and I taste her tears as the water pounds my back. I want to take her hard against the wall but she's demanding something slower, under her terms, and I resign myself to give her that much. Her small hand cups my face, dragging me closer to her and I pause our kiss so I can look into her blue eyes.

"Scarlett." I try her name out and it's funny, but it suits her. When I press my lips against hers she kisses me back and I already notice the shift between us. It's something deeper than flesh and I'm ready to step away from her. To step away from this. Her other hand reaches in and touches my cock and I lose myself in her touch. She strokes it and I reach out and touch the shower tiles. Blood drips off my face and hits the white tiles under our feet. I know I should try to stop the wound from bleeding but her touch is weakening me. Her strokes grow faster and I don't want to cum so easily, but I don't move. I give her whatever it is she needs from me right now. The loss of her hand has me looking at her. She's staring up at me, her hand cups one side of my face, her fingers tighten on my beard. The way she looks at me makes my heart pound faster. I have no idea if she wants to fuck me or kill me. I'm way too fucking pumped to see which it is.

Her anger ignites something in me that recognizes it.

"Say my name again." Her red lips move and I reach for her, wanting her closer, but she takes a step away from me while releasing my beard.

My cock throbs with a want for her.

"Scarlett," I say her name.

"Lie down."

Gladly. My body aches and standing is a chore. I lie down on the cold tiles. The water beats down on top of my chest, the warm water pours off me. Scarlett steps over me, her legs on either side of my body, and when she moves down, she grabs my cock and places it at her entrance.

It's my turn to gasp as she sits on my cock before rising back up and she starts to ride it. My hands hold her hips, but I don't guide her. I just let her fuck me. I'm too close to cumming already. I'm watching her body through a spray of water. Her face is twisted in ecstasy, her head is thrown back as she moves faster on my cock. Her whole body rising up, each time I think she's ready to get off me, she slams back down. My hands tighten on her hips as she continues to pump my cock. I want to take control, I want to bend her over but I know I need to allow her to have this. I can fuck her my way later. Her hand touches the tiles as she continues to drag herself up and down my cock.

She repositions herself until she's straddling me. Moving forward she moves through the spray, her pussy continues to grind at my cock and I move her body up and down, increasing the speed. Her hands sink into my hair and I'm looking into the bluest eyes I have ever seen. For the first time I don't see any fear in Scarlett. I just see a beautiful woman who's fucking me. My cock twitches as she moves down harder and I explode inside her, she cries out her own release and we ride the waves slowly. Her heavy breaths brush against my neck as she collapses on my chest. My hands instantly leave her hips and I wrap my arms around her. I'm dizzy from cumming and every ache I had returns with a vengeance. I have no idea how I'll get up, but a part of me would die happy here.

"Scarlett," I try out her name again.

"Hmmm." She's drifting off. I wonder if she has a concussion from the car crash.

"Scarlett, don't fall asleep."

She raises her head and looks at me, her eyes have grown sleepy. Her gaze trails across my face. "You're still bleeding."

I'm tempted to touch my head, but I don't unravel my arms from around her waist. "I know, but could you give me just another minute here? I think I like you in my arms."

The smile on her face is slow. "You do?"

My stomach twists and I have no idea why I like her words so much. I mirror her smile. "I do."

She smiles and lies back down taking all that sunshine with her. My hands tighten further on her and the idea of letting her go is something I don't think I will ever accept. My lips kiss the crown of her head.

"Don't fall asleep." I warn her again. She raises her head off my chest.

"Yeah, the water is getting cold." She's right, it is.

She's smiling again. "You need to let me go so I can get up."

"Never." I tell her and her smile shrivels away and the moment we share fades away and the gray of my life pours back in. I don't want it to end.

"Never." She repeats the word with a frown and I have no answer for her, only "Never." And I don't think she wants to hear that again, so I release her and she gets up.

"Any chance of helping me up?" I ask. She's staring down at me with all her perfect curves, before she steps out of the shower. I laugh, staring at the ceiling, as she leaves me bleeding on the ground. I remember waking up in the car to find my seatbelt undone. She hadn't left me to die. No matter what she thinks, she cares for me and she wants to be here. I just need her to understand why.

I groan as I roll onto my knees before pulling myself up. Pain strikes my head and I close my eyes. Swaying, I brace against the wall.

"Dean." Her voice has me smiling against the pain.

"I thought you left me to bleed to death," I say while keeping my eyes closed.

"If you die, then so do I."

I open my eyes and she wavers before my vision rights itself. Her eyes are slowly filling up with anger, but it's not as heavy as it normally is.

I leave the shower while holding onto the wall, and she watches me.

"Sit down." She points at the toilet and it feels like it's miles away. I manage to get to it. A warm towel is thrown across my shoulders. Scarlett has wrapped herself in a towel and she kneels in between my legs.

"I think I like you there," I say, while trying to stay conscious.

"This might sting." Her warning comes with agony and I tighten my fists to stay still.

I'm fucking awake now. "Jesus Christ." I grit and she stops. "Don't stop." I open my eyes and see fear that's started to tinge her eyes. "Don't stop." I repeat and she continues to clean my face, the stinging subsides slowly and I observe her as she works on my cut.

She has a freckle close to her right eye and I find myself wanting to kiss it. She bites her bottom lip, turning it red against her pale skin. Her eyelashes are dark and long, they shoot up as she looks into my eyes. My stomach twists and it's an odd sensation.

"Sing for me." Her eyes flutter closed and she shuts me out. I close my own eyes and let her work on my wound. Her fingers work quickly and softly. Then she starts to sing and it's haunting.

Nobody left, no calling birds.
The world departed, where is God?
Your taunts arise, on deaf ears they fall,
What is left? Is this truly all?
Move one step, take two back,

raw throat, a broken heart.
Who will cry? Oh, cry for me.
Landscape broken, set me free.
Freedom given, the price you pay.
No turning back, not today.

I can't look away from Scarlett as she sings, tears blur her eyes and her lips turn down as she continues to sing.

What to do? What to say?
One more chance, today's the day.
Rest your head, the sun will shine,
upon your face, you are divine.
Goodbye to you, you're sadly missed.
I will cry, I grant your wish.
A wish bestowed the day you died,
Oh young man, here comes the tide.
Don't you worry, I'll always be there.
Hands in hands, I'll treat them fair.
I'll watch upon the ones you love,
Don't you worry, fly, white dove.
Soar high, among the clouds.
But don't forget, to come back down.
Give guidance, a ray of light.
A small gesture, a touch so light.
Always cherished, always there,
our love for you will never falter,
this I swear.

She ends on a long sad note and my heart is beating rapidly. It's her ability to tell a story with her voice that has blown me away. There is also something personal in what she sang to me.

"Is that your song?" I ask when she pushes a bandage against my head.

"Yes." Her gaze flickers to mine and her cheeks heat up.

"You wrote it?"

Her lips tighten together and she nods before speaking. "Yeah."

She tapes the bandage before sitting back. "I think that should work." I don't care about my head.

"Who's it about?" I want to know about Scarlett.

"A neighbor who took his life and left his children behind."

"Did you know him well?" Why am I getting jealous? Why do I want him to die all over again?

"I used to babysit for him." She stands up and I can see the upset in her eyes.

"If I died, would you write a song for me?"

She stares at me before tightening her towel around her. "No," she answers as she leaves the bathroom.

CHAPTER EIGHTEEN

SCARLETT

I think Dean will feature in all my future songs, but I will never tell him that. I'm smiling as I enter our room and start to take the new clothes from the bags. He went shopping for me. I love the soft material on my skin. There is a moment that I feel something that resembles happiness, but, I know that's wrong. I shouldn't feel this emotion. It doesn't belong in the chaos of this place.

Dean enters the room naked and I can't take my eyes off him. His body is powerful. My stomach tightens and it's not just with pleasure, but fear. Fear that I am starting to feel something for someone who kidnapped me. I need to keep reminding myself of that fact. His heavy, dark eyes land on me as he pulls on boxers and then a pair of combat trousers.

"Not even a bad one?" He asks.

"What?" I have no idea what he is talking about. Have I missed something?

"Wouldn't you even write a bad song about me?"

He is getting hung up on this and I am secretly enjoying it. He wants me to write a song about him.

"I don't know Dean, I'd need to know more about you." I don't smile—I want to—when a look of concentration crosses his handsome face. He nods and pulls on a jumper.

"Okay, Scarlett."

I'm surprised when he walks up to me and places a kiss on my lips. "Put on your jacket."

I'm already shrinking back. I don't want to go outside. Bad things happen when we do.

"Put on your jacket." He repeats before leaving the room.

I finish getting dressed and pick up the army jacket he purchased for me. I have no idea how afraid I should be. Has he changed his mind about keeping me? Is he going to let me go?

Never.

I shiver and walk to the kitchen where he waits for me. He's dressed for the outdoors. A small backpack sits on the counter along with a larger one. My stomach squeezes. What is this?

Dean walks to me and I don't move as he pushes a black wooly cap onto my head.

"Let's go." He grabs the packs, and like an obedient dog, I follow. He covers the keypad, but I listen to the very distinct sound each digit makes. Four digits. My stomach quivers as the suction from the door sends a shiver racing across my skin. We leave the comfort of the bunker and climb the stairs.

"Are you going to kill me?" I ask, my hand reaching for my neck. I want my pendant. Saliva pools in my mouth and I feel the weight of the world on my shoulders. My body feels heavier as I climb the steps. My fists tighten as I think about what he keeps doing. I want to scream, 'just do it already!'

We reach upstairs.

"No." His answer is abrupt as he stops in what must be a living space. It's void of everything. There are only four walls, two large windows, and a door that leads out into the hallway.

"This would be a beautiful room." He's glancing around the space, and I suppose it would be, but my interior design mode isn't exactly kicking in. I want to know what is in the long bag. I think it's a sword. He's going to cut me up. Dean's dark eyes land on me and my heart rate escalates. He takes a step closer to me.

"You look pale." He frowns, like he can't for the life of him understand why.

"What's in the bag?" I point at it and his eyes skip to the army green bag on the ground.

"You'll see." He looks unsure as he scoops it up and I follow him outside. A bird circles above us and I watch it fly away. I want to scream at it to come back and let me escape with it.

"You want me to kill him?"

Dean is watching me. "What?"

"You hate birds. Do you want me to kill it?"

I glance at the bird as it gets farther away and I hope it never stumbles across Dean. "It's only a bird. I'm afraid of it, that doesn't mean I want it dead," I say, looking at Dean.

"Are you a tree hugger?" He hoists the sword bag up on his shoulder.

"Are we chopping down trees?"

His laughter makes all the hairs rise on my body. It's so unexpected and I'm transfixed on him.

"No, we aren't. Come on." He holds out his hand for me to take and I stuff my hands into my pockets. He isn't offended as he starts walking to the tree line.

Don't go into the forest with him, Scar, I warn myself. Every crazy serial killer chops up his victims in the forest. I swallow, maybe not all, but Dean isn't stable. How many other bodies litter the floor under my feet?

He's whistling and I'm ready to bolt when he stops and turns to me. He drops one bag and moves the sword one to the front. He unzips it and I'm screaming at myself to move as he pulls out a long black rifle. It is the same one I had seen him use on the roof of the building. The day he had killed the jogger. The day my life changed.

He strokes it like it's a pet and my abdomen tightens.

"The first time I held a rifle, I was terrified, but it also gave me such a sense of peace." He holds it now and looks through the lens before glancing up at me. "My mind is silent when I do this; it's the only time I really feel peace."

"By taking a life?" I question.

He smiles again and my heart jumps. "Funny, isn't it?"

No.

He holds out the gun for me. "Hold it."

I'm ready to step away, but I think twice, he's handing me a gun. The moment I grip it, his smile widens. "Don't try to shoot me, Scarlett."

I pull the gun but he doesn't release it, his fingers brush mine. "I'm not going to hurt you, but I don't want you to hurt me either."

My heart pounds against my chest. Is this a truce for now? I would be stupid to say no.

"Of course." His laughter makes me frown, it sends waves rippling across my skin.

"I don't believe you," he says, but releases the gun. The rifle is heavy and I look down the slick barrel. I look up from the gun and he comes fully into focus. He opens the backpack and takes out a green roll that, placing it on the ground. His eyes move up to me and I hold the rifle pointing at his chest. My heart beats too fast and blood roars in my ears as my finger dances over the trigger.

He's looking at me and there is no fear, but disappointment in his eyes. Would he have handed me a loaded gun? Think Scarlett—gain his trust and don't be stupid. I move the gun away from his chest and look through it again.

"It's cool," I say, looking up at him.

He's still watching me. "You should never point a gun at someone unless you intend to kill them."

I swallow and nod. "Okay." I feel the loss immediately when he removes the rifle from my hands and I wonder if I've made a terrible mistake by not shooting him.

"Lie down." He points at the plastic green roll on the ground. My chest tightens. Is he going to kill me now? I'm picturing my dead body being rolled up in the plastic.

I'm ready to plead when he lies down on the plastic. "It keeps our clothes clean." He glances back at me, and I blink tears that I quickly wipe away, as I try to stop my heart from ripping out of my chest. I lie down beside him. The heat of his body has me moving closer. He isn't going to kill me. More tears fill my eyes and I try to focus and not make a sound as he sets up the rifle.

"I used to spend hours lying still and waiting for the perfect shot. I've always liked my own company. I can be pretty funny." He glances at me and grins, but his smile leaves his face.

"Why are you crying?"

"I thought you were going to cut me up and wrap me in the plastic," I answer, and wipe my face.

His eyes roam across my face. "No. I'm just showing you what I like to do. You wanted to get to know me."

I look out into the trees. He is staring at me like I am making up stories. Like he didn't kidnap me and try to shoot me before.

"Okay." I manage to squeeze out and the rifle appears in front of me.

He shuffles closer and moves one hand over the rifle, the other he places close to the trigger. "Relax your shoulder." His breath fans out across my cheek. I turn and my lips nearly brush his—he's that close.

"Don't distract me, Scarlett." His voice has grown deeper.

I look into the lens of the rifle. "Now what?"

"Just take in what you see. I want you to really feel the rifle under your fingers."

He moves away and I feel the loss of his warmth straight away. I do as he asks. The gun is cold under my hand but I know it's a weapon that can do so much damage. There is power in touching it, but it also leaves me with an uneasy feeling.

"How do you feel?" The excitement in his voice has me looking at him. It's the first time I've seen him genuinely excited and realize he's sharing something with me that's important to him.

"Wrong," I answer him and sit up.

His excitement dwindles.

"Dean, thank you for showing me this, but I don't think I could ever kill someone."

His laughter has my eyes widening and my temperature spiking.

"What's so funny?" I can feel the heat in my cheeks.

His dark eyes return to me but I can still see the laughter in them. "I only let you look through the lens. No one mentioned killing someone. But that's all that's on your mind." He reaches out and touches my forehead. "Who are you picturing killing?"

His finger runs down the length of my face and I shiver under his touch. "No one."

You.

"I don't mind you lying to me anymore, Scarlett. Do you know why?"

I shake my head as his hand runs to my neck. "Because I know when you are lying."

His fingers jump from the vein that pulses through my neck.

"I scare you." It's not a question but a confirmation of the obvious. "Yet, you are attracted to me." His lip tugs up slightly. "You want to kill me." His grin widens and his fingers dance along my pulse. "Yet, you pulled me out of the car."

I swallow as my eyes skip to the bandage on his head.

"You told me your name." He's not teasing, his eyes have softened and my lips tug down as he stares at me. "You gave it willingly." He moves closer and I can't breathe as he leans in and places the softest kiss on my lips. "Thank you."

I nod, unable to find words.

"If I didn't bring you here, do you think you could have liked someone like me?"

I blink and tears spill. I'm choking on too much fear, and I try to push it away. This is all bizarre but I try to calm myself by taking a few deep breaths. Dean doesn't say anything and his hand rests on my neck.

"No," I answer, and his laughter does that funny thing to me again. When he smiles, I mirror it through my tears.

"I think I like when you lie to me."

Dean's hand tightens on my neck and I fear this is where he switches to the crazy person, but he releases me and looks out into the forest. I see what he is looking at, it's a deer. I don't dare move. It's looking right at us, it's frozen, and I've never seen one up close. The deer is bigger than I thought it would ever be. Dean is moving so carefully towards the rifle. It takes me a second to piece it together.

I clap my hands, the noise as loud as a gunshot and the deer races away.

"Why did you do that?" Dean's brows drag down.

I sit taller. "Why would you kill it?" Now I think how stupid my question is. He kills people, a deer would mean nothing to him. "Because I can."

"Just because you *can* do something doesn't mean you *have* to. It's cruel."

He's staring at me and I know the moment he decides he's shared enough. I try to think about what he is doing here, he's trying to share himself with me and I'm knocking it each step of the way. I feel conflicted about what I'm feeling for him. He starts to pack up and I can't take my eyes off his back. I shouldn't feel sorry for him.

"Your aim is exceptional." I reach for a compliment.

He puts the gun in the bag. "I know. Otherwise I wouldn't be a sniper." His dark gaze swing around to me. "Get up."

I quickly move off the green tarp as he rolls it up. "You can't get mad at me because I don't like you shooting a deer."

He pauses. "You said you wanted to know me. This is me." He continues rolling up the tarp.

"You told me that holding the gun gave you peace."

He pushes the plastic into the bag. "Yes, it does." He answers without looking at me.

"Peace from what?"

He pauses and glances at me before standing taller. "My mind, it's noisy."

I can see that. I wouldn't like to see inside his head.

I nod; not sure what to say.

"It's kind of funny." He's smiling again and I can't help but notice how handsome he is, and think if we had met under different circumstances, how building something with him would have been a pleasure.

"You stop the noise in my head."

My heart picks up and soon turns into a full out gallop. I stop the noise in his head. I'm smiling again and I let myself smile—like, really smile.

He drops the bag he's holding and steps up to me. "So, you're like my rifle."

I laugh and his eyes widen in surprise. "Don't compare me to a gun." A gun that spilt so much blood, my smile wobbles.

He captures my hand in his. "I like the peace that Scarlett brings to me."

I frown at him, not sure how his words are making me feel. I'm happy I give him peace but I shouldn't feel that way. I should want him to swim in despair.

"So, thank you." He pulls me closer and I have to crane my neck back to keep looking at him.

"Why don't we put the rifle away for a while, since you don't need her right now?" I ask and I'm aware of what I'm asking, but if maybe I could save a life when I couldn't save my own, then my bravery for this moment would count towards something.

He's staring at me. "If I did that, what would you do for me?"

I had thought me giving him peace was a trade-off already. "What do you want?"

His answer is quick. "Stop trying to kill me."

I'd laugh at the madness of this, but for now, I try to stay in this moment. He will put down his gun if I agree. I will try to escape—but for now—I think I would struggle to kill him anyway.

"Okay, I won't try to kill you if you put away your rifle."

His lips touch mine and I'm still not used to this kind of contact. It's so gentle that I want to run from it. "We have a deal, Scarlett."

"We have a deal, Dean."

CHAPTER NINETEEN

DEAN

I like the sound of her laughter. I haven't touched Scarlett in a few days; she seems to move around me more freely, and I can't get enough of it. I want her so bad but I don't want to erase the smile from her face. She's funny, that wasn't something I expected.

I enter the bedroom to find it empty. Her bed is made up on the floor and I hate that. I want her in my bed, but she asked me for this, and in return, she said she would consider writing a song about me. So I agreed.

The silver chain feels heavy in my hands. As I push open the bathroom door, she's wrapped in a white towel, and when she looks at me, all I want to do is touch her.

She tightens her hold around the towel but relaxes slightly when I don't enter. I look away from her but stay on the threshold.

"I thought you were dressed," I say, peeking at her.

She's still watching me. She looks tiny in the white towel. "I was just about to. Is there something you want?"

Her question carries a note of teasing and I face her, leaning my shoulder against the doorframe. Her gaze roams over my bare arms and I grin at her. "I want to give you something."

Her gaze returns to mine and I see her frown. She does that when she's uncertain about what she's feeling.

I step into the bathroom and watch the pulse in her neck grow faster. "Turn around."

She does without question. She turns away from me and I reach out and scoop up her wet hair, before letting the pendant dangle down in front of her. She doesn't move as I let her hair go and fasten her father's pendant around her neck. My hands slide to her shoulders and the feel of her skin under my hands has me closing my eyes. I should have never taken it from her.

She swallows and I feel her shoulders shake under my touch. I don't release her. I caused that pain in her, and now I'll stand here and let it leak onto me.

She turns, forcing my hands off her shoulders. Her ocean eyes rage with pain and I fucking hate it.

"Thank you." Her lip trembles as she speaks. "Can I have a moment?"

I hate that she wants me to leave. I want her to seek comfort in me, but she doesn't. I nod and leave her alone.

I focus on making her favorite sandwich for her. I take my time cutting the banana and coat it with sugar. She arrives into the kitchen and she keeps touching her neck. I can see the silver chain under her top. Her eyes are rimmed red and when she looks at me she wears that haunted look again but it's not as bad as it used to be, so I am taking it as a win.

I place the plate beside the notepad and pen that she gazes at now.

"I want something in exchange," I say, and her face grows tight.

She's so strong. She nods. "What do you want?" It's like she doesn't expect it for nothing, and I hate that too. She sits down and opens the sandwich. Heat colors her cheeks before she looks up at me.

"I want you to write down your full name."

"Why?" Fear makes her words shake.

I push the notepad towards her. "Please."

She grabs the pen in her left hand and writes her full name. Scarlett Cadwell.

She slides the notepad back to me and I stop her.

"I want the last address of where you lived with your auntie."

She frowns and pulls the notepad back towards herself. "I want something in exchange."

I hide a grin. "Name it."

"I want to swim in the rain."

"Scarlett." I dip my head forward. What she is asking for isn't possible.

She pushes the notepad with her full name scrawled across it towards me. "Then no address."

I fight yet another grin. "Okay."

The sandwich stops at her lips and she tilts her head. "Don't lie to me." Her voice is small.

"I've never lied to you." I say back.

She's staring at me and I don't mind. I like her attention. She grabs the pen and starts to write her address. I try not to snatch it up when she slides it to me.

"I hope you aren't lying to me." I tap the page.

She shrugs and takes a bite of her sandwich. "Maybe I am."

I grin this time, loving her playful tone.

I need to get another vehicle if I am to take her swimming in the rain. I also need to find out when the next downpour will be.

"You don't make it easy on me." I'm still smiling and she touches her top, I know under it lies her pendant.

"You never made it easy on me." She's half smiling—half breaking and it kills me.

I wait a few beats before asking my question. I want her to enjoy her sandwich. She doesn't mind me sitting beside her anymore and just watching her. I think she's gotten used to me. "Why do you want to swim in the rain?"

She smiles and licks sugar off her small fingers. Fingers that I know feel good around my cock. I try to keep my mind focused.

"It's hard to explain. I think it would be a moment of seeing mother nature at her finest. You know, to stand in the waves fully clothed, while the rain pelted you. I've often dreamt of it."

"Why have you never done it?" The beach is an hour away. It wouldn't have taken much to get there.

"I always said when I had my own place I would, because if I did it before then, what would I have to dream about?" She looks so fucking sad.

"You consider here your own place?" Something in me swells.

She laughs. "No." Her word hangs on laughter that sounds like I'm ridiculous for saying such a thing. "I just might never get to have my own place, so I need to stop waiting."

I'm up and ready to walk away from her because I can't stop the heaviness that's settled on my chest. This is happening to me lately, and I am starting to think something is wrong with my heart. I could be on the verge of having a heart attack. The thought of what would happen to Scarlett if I died, has me tightening my fists.

"Dean." Her voice is so fucking soft behind me.

"7610." I recite the code.

She doesn't ask me what it's for. There is a beat before I turn around and look into her wide ocean eyes.

"There is a safe in the gun room. The combination 7610. Inside is a phone. The code for the door is saved on it, under the contact, named door."

Her chest rises and falls rapidly and a shaky laugh leaves her mouth. "I thought it was the code for the door."

I can't smile back at her, because I feel like such a fucking monster. Right now, it's the best I can offer her. "Come on."

I leave the living space and enter the gun room. Walking to the wall, I move the picture aside so she can see the safe. I step back and let her look.

"I'll keep the door locked for now." I hate doing it, but obviously she'll try to run the moment I'm asleep.

"Any chance of telling me where you will store the key?" Her voice carries laughter and I move the picture back, cutting off the safe.

"It's not funny, Scarlett. If I die, you don't want to get stuck down here."

She chews her lip. "Are you sick?"

"No. Maybe." I'm not sure. Scarlett takes a step towards me, her small hand wraps around my bare arm and I love the feel of it on my skin.

"Dean, what's wrong?" her concern has me contemplating telling her the truth.

"I'm not sure."

She frowns and steps even closer to me. "You have to tell me. I'm your responsibility."

I grind my teeth. "I know that, that's why I'm telling you all this."

Her cheeks heat and she doesn't speak.

"I get a tightness in my chest. I think it's a sign of a heart attack."

Her laughter has me regretting telling her. "I'm sorry. But... I mean that's not a sign of a heart attack. It could be stress."

She lets me go and I fold my arms across my chest. "I didn't realize you were a doctor."

She grows serious. "Fair enough. The next time it happens, I want you to think about what just happened before your chest grew tight."

I think back to the episode that was only a few moments ago and think about her saying she would never own her own place.

I reach for her and press my lips against hers, not wanting to think. I just want to feel her. She reaches up and grips my shoulders, and it's all I need for my cock to grow hard.

Just like that, her touch silences all the noise in my head and she consumes me. The coconut body wash will be forever the smell I associate with Scarlett. I lift her up and she moves easily wrapping her legs around my waist. She's light to carry from the room and I open my eyes to see where I am going, but don't break the hungry kiss. She wants this as much as I do, and that makes me devour her lips even more.

When we land on the bed, she opens her eyes, and she looks dazed as she takes in her surroundings, like she can't fathom how she got here. Her gaze snaps to me as I drag her top up, I pause, allowing her a moment to stop me. I'm praying she doesn't. I'm not sure how much restraint I have left. She doesn't stop me and I remove the top along with her bra, letting her breasts free. She hisses as I take each one in my mouth. Her nipples grow hard and my cock throbs for release. I let her nipples go and pull off her trousers and panties. Her small fingers work quickly on my trousers. It's not quick enough for me so I remove everything. She has a brief moment to take me in but I can't stop the want that has me pinning her arms down and positioning myself in between her legs. My cock rests at her opening and the ache in me burns.

"Wait." Scarlett's breathy word has me pausing, it's like holding back an ocean. I need to go away now, but her arms are wrapped around my neck.

"Go slowly."

She's fucking serious. She has to see the strain on my face. I nod and inch in painfully slowly. Her eyes widen with each inch I take and I want to slow it down even further to keep seeing the pure amazement on her face. I remind myself that I'm causing that. When I'm fully in, I drag my cock slowly back out and she clings to me, her gaze bores into mine and my own excitement turns to something I don't understand. It courses through my body and it's fragile, like if I look away from her ocean eyes, I will lose this connection with Scarlett. She throws her head back as I go slightly faster.

"Don't look away," I say and her gaze diverts back to me. It's in her eyes, a wonder, but something so much deeper. I'm moving faster and her eyes grow bigger and more glazed over, slowing down has them burning with ecstasy. I realize that I could do this for a while, just to watch her. It's fascinating, so I do. I continue to enter her slowly.

"Go faster," she pleads, and I do. I speed up and the ecstasy grows on her face, she's so wet around my cock and when her nails sink into my shoulder, I know she's close to cumming. I allow myself to let go and pound into her, my own release isn't far away and when she cums while looking into my eyes, I empty myself. I feel it leave me and enter her and I can't stop looking at her as I pump the last few times.

I slow down and stop and I want to ask her what was that? I'm not sure I want to do that again. It left me feeling exposed. I pull out of her and Scarlett doesn't move as I lie beside her before dragging her body into mine. My chin rests on her head, her back rises and falls as she continues to catch her breath.

"I got around to writing you that song."

My heart slams into my chest. "Can I hear it?"

I want to hear it. I want to hear how she sees me. "It's not finished yet." She sounds unsure and I want to see her face, but I'm not ready to face her yet. My body is still reeling from what we just did. It wasn't fucking. I'm not exactly sure what it was, but I push it away and drag her closer to me.

CHAPTER TWENTY

SCARLETT

It's weird as I move around his kitchen. I asked him to wait on the couch and watch some TV, but he's sitting at the kitchen table watching me cook.

"Remember your promise."

I glance over my shoulder at him, while holding the wooden spoon over the pot, so none of the tomato soup drips onto the stove.

"What promise?" I'm trying to think of what promise I made to him.

"That you won't try to kill me." His lip tugs up slightly but his eyes tell me he's very serious.

I stir the pot. "You think I'm going to poison you?" I question before taking a taste. I cough. It needs more salt. "You could be right." My heart jumps as his strong hands clutch my waist.

"I like you in my kitchen."

I bite my lip. I like being in his kitchen and that scares me. How long will this last—until he doesn't like me in his kitchen? Over the past few days, I haven't thought about escaping.

"What are you thinking?" He leans in, his beard scratching my cheek.

"I'm thinking it needs more salt." As I manage to move past him, his hands slide from my waist and I feel the loss immediately.

Dean returns to the table and sits back down. I finish up the soup and each time I glance at him, he's watching me. I hate how nervous I feel as I walk with the soup to the table.

"If you don't like it, you don't have to eat it," I say, placing the bowl and spoon in front of him. He digs in straight away and when he glances up at me, his smile is warm.

"I like it."

I duck my head, hoping to hide my stupid smile as I scoop up a spoonful of soup. It is nice.

"Who taught you how to make it?" Dean asks. His bowl is nearly empty.

"My auntie. She worked night shifts in the hospital, so it was a healthy meal that didn't require too much work."

I take another spoonful, and I'm there. Back at the wooden table, glancing up at the plasma on the wall. I hate the island behind me. It always holds some alcohol that he either started to drink or finished. I never touch it, but I know it's there. My soup warms my stomach and when I flicker a glance at Dean, he's watching me again.

"What?" I ask as my stomach squirms.

"You're different."

I laugh, it's not a belly laugh, it's abrupt and I'm just grateful that I have no soup in my mouth or it would be spewed everywhere.

"What exactly are you comparing me to? All the other females you have kidnapped?" The words are out of my mouth and I want to stuff them back in. His fist tightens around the spoon.

"You're the only person I've ever taken."

Lucky me. I have nothing good to say to that, so I eat more of my soup.

"Why can't you just take a compliment?" His words sound angry.

I glance back up at Dean and I see hurt on his face. Like I hurt him for telling him the truth about the situation. I don't want to imagine what it would feel like to have someone like Dean really favor me over other women. I would be flattered, but this isn't a normal situation.

"Because it's not a compliment." I stand, my stomach growing sour with what he is confronting me with. "This isn't normal." I tell myself out loud as I place the bowl and spoon in the sink. "This isn't right." I tell the sink.

"This isn't my home. You didn't pick me." I'm ranting but I'm choking.

My heart leaps as his hands touch my waist. I hadn't heard him move.

"Let's go for a drive."

I close my eyes and take a deep breath. "I don't want to go outside today, Dean."

"What *do* you want?"

He asks the question like he might give me what I want. My freedom, I want to tell him, but, I'm not stupid—that won't happen.

"I want to be alone." My heart beats faster and his hands slide from my waist. I turn to find the room empty. Guilt churns in my stomach for sending him away.

After a while, I decide that I don't want to be alone. I hate my thoughts. I hate how I want to see him. I find Dean in the gym and I stay at the threshold as he does pull-ups on a bar. He has no top on and I watch all those muscles coil and tighten with each lift.

He pauses in the middle of one of his pull-ups before he continues. It's the only tell that he knows I'm here.

"How many can you do?"

He drops down and turns to me. My core tightens as sweat makes a path down his chest. I try to keep his gaze, but fail.

"One hundred." He picks up a towel and wipes away some of the sweat. "Do you want me to prove it?" He asks.

I can't stop the smile. "No. I believe you." His body tells me that he works out a lot.

He sits down on a weight bench and picks up a weight. "You can join me if you want."

I prefer watching him, but I step into the room.

"Don't try to kill me." He sounds so serious.

"Didn't I already tell you I wouldn't? You can't keep bringing it up."

I love the sound of his laughter. "I can keep bringing it up. It's not every day the woman you live with keeps trying to kill you."

Live with? He makes it sound like it is my choice. I push that thought to the back of my mind as I reach up and grip the bar. I try to pull myself up, my arms wobble and I touch the ground again. Dean puts down his weights and sits up. His dark eyes drink me in and I grip the bar and try harder. I shiver and shake but manage to get my chin above the bar.

"Do it again." he demands.

I glance at him and grip the bar and try to pull myself up again. I manage to do it, but it takes everything in me. Dean gets up and moves behind me.

He lifts me up easily as I grip the bar. "One, Two, Three..." I grin at him over my shoulder, our faces close. "I think that's cheating."

He grins back. "Who said?"

I laugh and when he lowers me to the ground, his hands remain on me, and I like it. I like the feeling of his hands on me. I like the smell of him, I like the smell of his home. I'm starting to feel something that resembles happiness here. I close my eyes and try to picture if this were my choice, how that might feel. I could be happy. I think of crossing that line and allowing myself to be happy right now. Turning in his arms, my stomach squirms as his dark eyes roam my face.

I want to tell him I could be happy with him, but I have no idea how he actually feels about me. He didn't pick me, he was forced to take me.

His fingers run up alongside my face and stop at my temples. I can see he wants to ask me something, but he hesitates. I don't blame him.

"You're different, too." My heart jumps into my throat after the words leave my mouth.

"Is that a good different or a bad different?"

His fingers move in circles.

I shrug. "Just different."

He nods like he gets it, his fingers work their way down to my neck.

"In a good way," I add.

His fingers stop, his gaze skips to mine. I can't decipher what's going through his head. Is he thinking I'm foolish? I'm showing him that I'm starting to care. That isn't wise. I need to remember why I am here and how I got here.

His lips crash on mine and it weakens me. I'm clinging to his sweat soaked chest. My hands rise up and circle the back of his neck. He breaks the kiss, his eyes skip across my face. I have no idea what passes in his gaze, I can't decipher the emotion.

I release him as an alarm I have never heard before rings out.

"What's that?"

Fear. That's what I read on Dean's face. He grabs his top and pulls it on as he rushes from the room and I'm on his heels as he enters the gun room. He removes a gun from the wall and punches the code into the safe, where he takes out a box of bullets.

"What is that?" I ask again.

He loads the gun without looking at me. "Someone is in the house.

Fear skitters up my back. "Like, here?" I'm pointing at the floor, but keeping my voice down.

He points at the ceiling. "Up there." He sticks the loaded gun into the band of his trousers. I follow him out the door. He locks the gun room behind us.

"Has this happened before?" I ask as I follow him into the kitchen. The screech of the alarm still blares and I want it to stop. It's causing my heart to race too fast.

"No." Dean looks around the space before going into the kitchen. He opens the cabinet under the sink and reaches inside it while looking at me. He pulls out a hunting knife, and everything stills in me as he stands up.

I don't want him to leave. "Just stay here, and whoever is up there will leave." I plead with him taking a step forward.

"No." He walks around me and I block his path again.

"Please, Dean."

"What are you afraid of? That I'll die up there and you're locked down here? Remember the code?"

I nod. But that's not why I don't want him to go up there.

"Tell me the code!" He barks.

"7610 but ..."

He steps closer to me. "If I don't return, wait until tomorrow before you leave, in case they are still up there."

I hear his words but they aren't registering. I'm not thinking of me getting stuck down here, I'm thinking of someone hurting him up there. I never get to tell him, because he places a kiss on my forehead and leaves. The moment the door closes, the alarm stops. My ears buzz in the silence and I wait for him to return.

CHAPTER TWENTY-ONE

DEAN

"How did you find me?" I keep the gun in my hand as Gage turns to me. He's in the hallway. My gaze skips to his empty hands.

"It wasn't hard." He has a few days growth of stubble.

"Are you trying to grow a beard?" I grin at him and also try to listen for anyone else. "Are you alone?" I fire quickly.

"I'm alone. I found a burnt up car, and have been searching this area. I've been here a few times, but it looked derelict." He glances around the hallway at the peeling paint and fading wallpaper.

"What do you want?" It was stupid of me to have left the vehicle so close to where I live, but it isn't registered in my name. I didn't think anyone would piece it together. Of course Gage did.

"Where's Kate?" He glances into the sitting room behind me.

"That's what you came for?" I push the gun into the band of my trousers. My trigger finger is feeling heavy and I don't want Gage to piss me off and make me shoot him.

Gage takes a step towards me, dark circles under his eyes look stark. "I came because you never came back and I had to go to the meeting myself." His jaw clenches.

"So, it's sorted?" I ask.

He grabs me by the collar of my shirt. "Are you fucking serious?!"

I shove Gage off me. "Yeah, I am."

He runs a hand down his face. "They want you. You shot a woman who had a connection to the Irish Mafia."

I shrug. "Fuck sake, Gage. I shoot a lot of people." Those words weigh heavily on my shoulders.

"Children?" He asks, then holds his hands up. "Don't tell me."

He glances behind me again. "Where's Kate? Did you kill her?" He's done waiting. He storms into the sitting room and I follow him in. He's facing the door. "What the fuck is that?" He glances at me. "Is she locked in there? What is it?"

"She's fine. You need to leave." My hand moves to the waistband of my trousers and Gage follows my hand.

"Or what? You'll shoot me?"

I grin at him. "It's very tempting."

"I know you don't give a fuck about me, but they paid dad a visit."

Blood drains from my body. "Is he dead?" I try to keep my breathing even.

"No, but they roughed him up."

I nod as relief allows the blood to re-enter my system.

Gage steps closer. "They hurt mam."

I can't look at him. He's blaming me. I shrug because I don't know what else to do.

"Do you care?" He shoves me and the strain is heavy in his eyes.

"I get you're upset, but don't touch me." He knows I don't like to be touched.

"Let the girl go and we might be able to fix this."

My stomach tightens. "Letting the girl go will do no good. You said it was over the woman I shot."

"But they are using the girl as a way to bring you out. So release her and give them one less reason. These people are fucking serious, Dean!" He curls his hands into fists and steps away from me again, he's back to glaring at the door.

"What the fuck do they want? I kill people. That's what I do!" I'm shouting, because I have no idea how to fix this.

"They set up another meeting in two days' time."

I glare at Gage and sneer. "I'm not going. I'll be clipped in a second."

Gage clears the space and shoves me into the wall. "If you don't show up, our parents will be their target. They won't stop at me, Dean, think of mam and dad. For one fucking second, think of someone other than yourself."

I shove Gage off me. "So what? I'm not a fucking martyr. I'm not going to die."

"You're a selfish bastard." He's facing the door again. "I want to see the girl."

I laugh now. What the fuck is his hang up with Scarlett? Does he like her? "No."

Gage pulls out a gun and I'm grinning. Honestly, I'm a little surprised that he has the balls to pull a gun on me.

"Open that door."

"No." I continue to grin.

He fires a shot into the ceiling, and I flinch. "Fuck sake, Gage! You'll attract attention."

He points the gun at the floor. "I'll empty the rest into the floor."

He knows he's won. I move faster than he expects, my gun pointed at his head. "If you do, I'll shoot you." I threaten, and it's his turn to grin.

"So, she is down there, and she must be alive."

He's watching me. "I already told you she's alive."

"I want to see her."

He has no idea how close I am to pulling the trigger, or maybe he sees it in my eyes as he slowly puts away his gun.

"What aren't you telling me?" I push the gun against his temple.

He growls at me, but wisely raises his hand. "I've told you everything. You've pissed off some pretty powerful people. Now I just want to save our parents' lives."

Letting Scarlett go might ease the anger of the people who want me dead, but they'll still want me dead. Also, I'm not giving her up. I take the gun out of my brother's face. The moment I do, his fist connects with my nose. The rush is instant as I bend over. Blood drips onto the wooden floor.

"This is a safe house?"

I glance up at Gage while holding my nose. I can only open one eye as pain radiates from my face.

"Yes." I grit out.

Gage nods as I stand straight and wipe blood from my face.

"I'm bringing mam and dad here. They'll be safe."

"Sure, why don't you come, too? We can sit down and have that family dinner we have always talked about." He is out of his fucking mind. My own mind skips to Scarlett sitting with my parents.

"I will."

I'm standing straighter. "I was joking."

"I'm not."

"What about Scarlett? How the fuck do I explain that?" I have to state the obvious. His grin has me clenching my fists.

"That's your problem. Expect us here in a few hours." He starts to walk away. "Also, maybe come up with a good cover story of why you have a safe house."

"Don't bring them back here!" I shout at Gage as a new panic starts to rise. I don't want people in my space. The front door slams and I'm staring at the wall.

Fuck.

I arrive into the kitchen and Scarlett isn't there. I'm not overly surprised. I'm waiting for her to charge or attack me with something, but I don't hear a sound. Taking the dish cloth, I run it under the cold tap and press it against my nose as I walk through my home. Is he really going to bring our parents here? How will I explain Scarlett? I can lock her up until we get this sorted. Two days. She'll only be locked away for two days. I can duct tape her mouth so she doesn't make any noise. Tie her to the bed.

I open the doors as I pass but each empty room has my stomach twisting. When I enter the bedroom, her tear soaked face glances up at me.

"What happened?" I drop the cloth and I'm gripping her face. Did Gage deceive me? Did someone hurt her while I was up there with him? She's not speaking and everything in me is crashing.

"What happened?" I squeeze her face tighter.

"I heard a gunshot..." Her words trail off as she sobs and I pull her into my chest. I can't think clearly as blood pumps too quickly around my body.

"I thought they shot you." She's whimpering and I pull her tighter to me. She is crying for me. She has been worried. She has been as worried about me as I have been about her. I plant a kiss on the crown of her head.

"I'm okay. I'm here." I smile into her hair and she clings to me. If I had been shot, she would have been stuck down here. That's what she is fucking crying over. It wasn't over me. It was being left here alone. I pull her tighter, burying her face against my chest. Her small hand taps my back and I close my eyes as I hold her tighter. I need to end her now, end her before she consumes me.

I tighten my hold on her until her slaps turn more frantic. I'm away from her and she's gasping and staring up at me. I push my hands behind my back, like I didn't just consider killing her.

Her hand goes to her neck and she fingers the pendant. I'm not sure if she's aware of it. Her mouth opens and closes as she stares at me. Right now, I hate her. I hate how beautiful she is at this moment—I hate that I can't kill her.

"Don't leave this room." I march from the bedroom and slam the door behind me. I'm glaring at it. Hoping she defies me. I don't hear a sound. Anger laces its way through my bloodstream and it's a cruel kind of anger. It's the kind that I need to unleash and I find myself walking away from the bedroom door because I don't want Scarlett to be the target. I don't want her to see the ugly inside of me.

Blood drips onto my lips and I re-enter the kitchen and grab a fresh dishcloth to try to stop the bleeding.

I could get rid of her before Gage arrives back with our parents. No doubt he will keep to his promise.

The fucking annoying part is that the woman was never meant to die. I was paid to kill two men, but my target had sent his wife. She had tried to kill my client and I had pulled the trigger. Job done. I wouldn't have intervened, but he's a friend of a friend. Now I realize my mistake for not just doing my job. This is what happens when you move outside the lines of a contract.

I have to make up my mind quickly. I either get rid of Scarlett or tell her the truth. I laugh into the sink. The truth? What the fuck is that anymore?

I glance over my shoulder, expecting to see her standing there, but the space is empty. What would it be like to have her gone? I don't like the thought at all. I'm moving again, and this time when I open the bedroom door, it hits the wall. She jumps, spinning around. I hate how beaten she looks. I need her gone. I need to erase her. She takes a step back and I wonder if she can see it in my eyes. That I need to turn this off. She turned it on inside me and now I need it turned off before it destroys both of us.

CHAPTER TWENTY-TWO

SCARLETT

F ear skitters up my back. My brain is on a loop that he tried to smother me. His eyes hold violence that I don't want to be on the receiving end of. I have no idea what's happened from the man who placed a kiss on my head, to this.

"What's wrong?" My voice trembles as he steps closer. His gaze doesn't leave my face and I bite the inside of my jaw. What had I done? I'm trying to think, and my brain scatters in too many directions.

"People are coming."

I swallow the sob. I knew this would come. I knew he would kill me, but was I being loaned out to people? "What kind of people? Are they going to hurt me?" It's better to know.

"Just people." His irritation has him running his hands through his hair, but that doesn't answer my question. *Are they going to hurt me?*

"I'm not sleeping with people," I say lamely, but the fear of being used is choking me.

He clears the space and I have no idea what's fueling this anger in him. His hand touches my neck, he doesn't tighten his hold, but he's struggling, I can see it.

I blink and tears spill. "I'd prefer to die."

My words have him pushing me away. I stumble but manage to keep myself upright.

I don't understand what's happened. I thought we were starting to like each other. I feel so foolish. I like him. I like the man who kidnapped me. It is more than like.

"It's three people. It will be for two days." Dean's pacing as he runs his hands through his hair.

Three people, two days. Numbers, but no answers. Are they going to hurt me? Is he going to allow them to hurt me? Panic has my feet moving and I step into his path and grab his face. He seems startled as I reach up on the tip of my toes and press my lips against his. His hands grip my face and his kiss is harsh and savage. We are moving, and when I sink onto the bed, I don't mind getting lost in this moment. My pain alters too quickly and I know his touch burns all the pain away. Dean's erection prods my stomach and I drag him closer. He breaks the kiss panting, his hot breath fans across my face as he looks down at me. I don't want him to look at me, I don't want him to see the struggle that tears through me. I grab his shirt, pull him to me, kissing him again and he returns it, but he doesn't close his eyes; his kiss is too gentle. I don't like it. I press my lips harder against his, but he doesn't get fired up like he had two minutes ago. My teeth sink into his lip and he quickly pulls away. I let him go as he gets off me. His fingers come away with blood from his swollen lip. His gaze bores into me as I lick his blood off my lips.

He's glaring at me. "They will be here in an hour."

I'm scurrying off the bed. People are really coming. I have no idea what will happen to me. I can't be expected to just wait. I have an hour.

I nod my head, as if I understand that this is how it works.

"Don't look at me like that!" His bark is loud and he's moving back to me. His hand circles my neck again.

"Do it." I push my body into his hand. "End it for me, because it would be easier this way."

His eyes trace my face, but he doesn't move.

My hands connect with his chest. "Do it!" My voice rises and I hit him again. "Do it, you fucking coward!"

He releases my neck and my hand connects with his face. The sound is like a gunshot in the room.

I'm choking on terror and I want it to end, but he stares at me with inky eyes.

"I hate you." I clear the space and hit his chest again. "I hate you!" I scream louder and lash out again. This time his hand circles my wrist and he drags me to his chest where he holds me and I sob, waiting for the pressure of his hand on the back of my head to come. He's going to smother me, and some broken part of me welcomes death. All I have to do is think of being shared around. That type of hurt is cruel and not worth the small joys of this world. Not to me, anyway.

"No one is going to hurt you." Dean's words break through my heartache and his hand that had been on the crown of my head, strokes my hair. My fists tighten on his shirt and I'm breaking all over again. I'm gasping and trying to stay up right. His hand circles my waist, like he knows I can't hold up my own weight anymore.

"No one will hurt you." He keeps repeating the words and it's funny because they start to calm the hysteria that is building inside me. I'm falling for him. That's the part that is making me cry harder. Shame burns my body—shame because I want him to comfort me, I want him to hold me.

"You can't tell them who you are."

I'm slowly coming out of my cocoon and trying to look up at him, but he keeps me pinned to his chest.

"If you tell them the truth, I'll have to kill you." His words are steady, but they hurt so fucking much. I need to remind myself that I'm falling for him; but to him, I'm a means to an end.

"Do you understand, Scarlett?"

Once again I try to look up at him, but he holds me firm.

"Yes." I bite out the word and clear my throat. Now he lets me go. A small blood spot rises from the puncture wound on his lip and I'm transfixed on it.

"Whatever I introduce you as, that's what you are." His lips move. I nod my head.

"If they ask you a question, let me answer."

I nod again, because no one will hurt me. He said it himself. That no one would hurt me. I can't take anymore hurt. "No one will hurt me," I say, and reach up dabbing at the blood on his lip, his tongue flickers out and touches my fingers that I withdraw.

"I won't let anyone hurt you." He holds my chin and I'm falling into his onyx eyes. "I'll keep you safe."

Who'll protect me from you? I nod. "Safe." What a foreign word. It sounds like the word hope, or faith, or even trust. Words that are thrown around, and yet to fulfil any of them, it takes something that's close to love.

I drop his gaze.

"Go get showered and cleaned up." He releases me and I can't move.

"Dean..."

His jaw is tight as he glares down at me. My fingers automatically go to my pendant.

"Yes?" He's waiting for me to speak, but I can't. What I want to ask is unreasonable, and I can't understand why I seek it now. I want him to come with me. I want his touch.

I shake my head, my face darkening from my own stupid thoughts.

"Nothing."

He holds me in his stare before releasing me with a nod. I quickly leave the room before I say something else that I won't be able to take back.

The water pours down on my back and I'm ready to cry, only now that I'm alone, no tears come. The fog that Dean's presence often wraps me in, disappears and reality sinks back in. Maybe this is why I wanted him with me. I didn't want my own personal thoughts coming back. Closing my eyes, I bow my head and let the water race down my back. I want to feel something other than this turmoil. I don't know what it is I want. I tighten my fists until my nails dig into my palms; the pain is instant, but it isn't enough. I clamp down on the inside of my mouth until I release it from the pain. A sob along with a dribble of blood pours from my mouth and I sink to the floor. Pulling my knees to my chest, I sit right under the spray of water.

I'm crawling across the shower until I reach my clothes. I glance up at the door and when no one enters, I tug on my top and trousers. It's hard enough getting into them, but I manage to. I'm grinning like a lunatic as I step back under the spray of water. My body trembles from the sudden warmth and I spin, as I visualize soaking myself under the spray of rain. I sit back down on the floor and let the rain soak my clothes. My hands tap on the ground to a beat that pulses in my body. I want to shout to the sky. I want to tell everyone who sees me to fuck off and keep walking. A laugh bubbles up my throat as I picture them, rushing past me wondering what the crazy girl is doing. I'm not crazy, am I? Small puddles of water are gathering as I sit on top of the drain. I splash and some part of me is elated at the noise. Red wellie boots spring to mind. Maybe I had a pair once. I have no idea, but the more I splash, the more my excitement grows.

"What are you doing?"

I scream as I open my eyes. Dean is looking down at me. I stop splashing and wipe water from my eyes. "Taking a shower."

I get up off the ground.

"In your clothes?"

"I..." I trail off. He wouldn't understand what I was doing. "I like the rain." I shrug.

"You need to be honest with me, Scarlett."

I nod like I'm always honest. *Don't laugh.* I swallow the laughter that wants to bubble up my throat.

"Are you okay?"

I can't stop the laughter that keeps pouring from my mouth. It keeps coming, and each time I look up at Dean to tell him to give me a minute, I can't speak as laughter silences my words. My laughter changes without my permission and I'm sobbing. I turn my back on him and bury my face in my hands, I don't want anyone to see me like this. Sobs render me speechless again, and I want him to go. I need to tell him I'm okay, it's just a moment, one small moment in the expanse of my life. How many moments have I lost to this pain? Too fucking many. Arms circle me and Dean's touch manages to break me further. I want this so badly, I hate how much I need him. I turn and he pulls me into his chest, where he lets me unleash all my pain.

I want to pin down this pain and be done with it, yet it just won't leave me.

"Scarlett, I need you to keep it together." Dean's words smash through my pain and I'm leaning out so I can look at him.

"You don't make it easy." I'm staring up at him.

A ghost of a smile touches his swollen lip. "I know."

His acknowledgment has me pulling myself a little bit more back together.

"I'm trying." I admit, but I'm struggling. He places a kiss on my lips and it's too gentle.

I try to grab him and pull him to me, but he encircles my wrists with his long fingers. His gaze bores into me and he doesn't say anything. All I can hear is the running water that soaks his back. I want to touch him, I want to run my hands into his beard, but he releases me and steps back. His brows draw down. "Get dressed." His command isn't delivered with his usual heaviness.

I nod and he leaves me. I step forward and return to the spray of water. I visualize what I always visualize. All the pain and anger is covering my body. The black substance starts to wash away under the spray of water. I help it by pulling off my clothes and letting it go down the drain, washing it all away. As I step out of the shower, I wrap myself up in a towel, and take several deep breaths. I need to keep it together. The sound of an alarm has everything in me freezing.

CHAPTER TWENTY-THREE

DEAN

I can't meet my dad's black eye. Gage helps mam down the steps. I can see the uncertainty that crosses her face. She looks older.

"You will be safe here." Gage smiles at her and she clutches his arm. White pearls around her neck look larger than I remember, or maybe she's smaller. My dad glances around the living space.

"It's nice." He declares while nodding his head. Purple bruises blossom on the back of his neck and I can't meet Gage's gaze. He's staring at me, but anger fills me far too quickly.

"Sit down." I've never had them in my home, so I'm not exactly used to hosting. "Can I get you a drink?"

Dad sits down, and the pain that crosses his face tells me that they didn't leave much of him untouched. The gray peaky cap, he pulls from his head.

"Anything strong?" His smile has me nodding as Gage helps mam to the couch.

She stops me and I struggle to meet her gaze. Her small hand touches my beard. "You need to shave." Small blue eyes that waver stare up at me. She's getting smaller. I feel like a giant beside her. My mam's gaze swings to Gage and she touches his face that has some stubble on it. "You too."

Gage nods and smiles at her. "I will, Mam."

For the first time I meet Gage's gaze and he raises both brows. "Where's your guest?"

"Getting dressed." I bite out.

"Oh, you have someone here?" My mam's interest has Gage smiling, but my insides rock and I push it down.

"Yeah." I leave them and pour out a brandy that I knock back before refilling it. I pour my dad a drink. Mam has never drunk a drop of alcohol in her life. When I hand dad his drink, he's glancing around the space.

"Why do you live underground?" He asks while taking a sip of his drink.

"Frank, not now." My mam tries to wave off his question. Gage removes his gray, long, coat before sitting down. He's enjoying this far too much.

"My job has me keeping my location a secret."

"A secret?" My mam's eyebrows rise into her hairline. "Yeah, I do secret things." I ramble and walk back to the kitchen area.

"He works for the government." Gage fills in my bullshit story as I make my mother a cup of tea. I knock back the glass of brandy before pouring out another. Gage is up and walking around. I want to tell him to sit the fuck down.

"Why didn't you come home for Christmas?" My mam asks the moment I place the tea in front of her.

"I got called away for work," I lie.

Her small eyes fill with understanding.

My dad is watching me. "You look good," he says.

My stomach squeezes as Gage makes his way out of the room. "What are you doing?" I ask.

He stops walking. "Just curious."

"Scarlett is getting dressed. Give her some privacy."

Gage holds up his hands, but his eyes flash with a question. "She's taking her time." He doesn't think she's here.

"That's a lovely name." My mam sips the tea and I can see the wheels turning in her head. Gage grins as he comes back to the couch and I want them all to leave. I can't do this. There's too many people.

"Hello." My dad speaks and I look up. Scarlett is standing in the kitchen area and she looks startled. Her gaze darts around everyone before they land on me. The pulse in her neck is visible, but I don't need to see it to know she's afraid. I walk to her, cutting them off. I'm hoping the warning in my eyes is enough that she doesn't start screaming. I clamp down on my own fear and twine our fingers together. Her small hand is damp in mine as I bring her to the couch. Once this part is over, it will get easier, I tell myself.

"This is Scarlett." Gage and my dad are focused on our joined hands. My mam is beaming up at me.

"This is my brother, Gage, whom you've met."

Gage nods his head and his eyes are filled with questions. I skip ahead to my mam.

"This is my mam."

I glance at Scarlett and she looks up at me with surprise on her face. I can see it in her eyes, the questions too. My mam rises off the couch.

"It's so lovely to meet you."

I release Scarlett's hand as she steps into my mam's embrace. "It's lovely to meet you, too." Scarlett's voice wobbles a bit, but she's doing good. My dad is watching me and I wait until my mother releases Scarlett.

"This is my dad." My dad approaches Scarlett. I don't think she's aware of what she is doing. Her hand reaches back and tightens around mine. I move her close to me. My dad reaches out his hand.

"Lovely to meet you."

Scarlett takes his outstretched hand and gives it a quick shake. "You too." Her voice is low, like she's tired after a day of socializing. I pull Scarlett back towards me, my gaze going to Gage, who hasn't taken his eyes off me. His jaw is clenched.

"Can I have a word?" He asks.

I'm not leaving Scarlett here with my parents. "Not right now." I try to pass it over.

Gage stands. "It will only take a minute. Scarlett can keep our parents company. She can tell them how you met."

Is he fucking serious? Is he trying to jeopardize everything?

Scarlett releases my hand and I feel the loss straight away. "It's okay." Her words are soft and I don't trust her for a second. I'm ready to threaten her, but I can't with everyone watching.

I lean in to brush a kiss on her lips. I hope it's enough to make her understand not to test me. "I'll only be a minute."

She nods, but I can't leave.

"We aren't going to eat the girl." My mam lets out an annoyed breath at all of us standing and no one moving. I exhale and meet her gaze with a smile.

"I know, Mam."

"Then go." She orders, and I meet Scarlett's eye one final time before I leave the room with Gage.

"Make it quick." I bite out once we are down the hall. I can hear the small chatter from my mam. She'll grill her with questions.

"What are you doing?" Gage stops me from walking.

I shake his arm off me. "Don't touch me, and that's my question to you. What the fuck was that in there? I'm trying to make this look normal."

Gage sneers. "Normal? What the fuck have you done to that poor girl? Introducing her as your girlfriend. She looks terrified."

"What do you want from me?" I shove him and his back collides with the wall, the noise is loud.

"Everything okay?" Dad appears at the end of the hall. His prodding eyes have Gage standing straight.

"Yeah, Dad. Just give us a minute."

Dad walks away and Gage is in my face. "You should have locked her up, not let her sit with our parents. Sometimes I fucking wonder about you, Dean."

I'm walking away because I don't want another second to pass where Scarlett has an opportunity to tell my parents she's been forced to stay here. Gage doesn't stop me. Scarlett is sitting beside my mam. I glance over my shoulder, but Gage hasn't followed me. Nosy bastard.

"Everything okay?" My dad asks again as I sit down beside Scarlett, who stops talking.

"Yeah, Dad. Gage is just being an asshole." I pick up the glass of brandy.

"Language." My mam corrects.

"Sorry." I mumble. I'm aware Scarlett is watching me. My gaze flicks to her and I can't for the life of me decipher what I see in her ocean eyes.

"So how long has this lovely lady been your girlfriend?" I can see my mother's excitement. I don't blame her. She's never met a friend of mine, never mind a girlfriend.

"A while." I scratch my beard and glance up at the hall. Where the fuck is Gage?

"You were just about to tell me how you met." My mam has turned her attention back to Scarlett. My dad watches her with interest. This is all starting to feel like a really bad idea.

"Why don't you tell them." Scarlett's smile wobbles. She looks tired. "Scarlett is a singer." My mam's face lights up. "She was singing at a bar and that was it, our eyes met and I had to bring her home."

Scarlett glares up at me and I lean in and press a kiss on her lips. I didn't have to, but her smell and her presence is keeping me stable right now.

"Sing us a song." My dad shuffles forward on the couch and Gage reappears.

"Maybe another time," I say and glance at Gage, who sits down.

"I didn't know you were a singer, Scarlett."

"Now you do." I finish quickly.

"Yeah, I sing for a living." Scarlett's voice sounds softer as she speaks to Gage, and when I look at her, she's wearing a genuine soft smile that I want to tear from her face. It dissolves when her gaze collides with mine.

"You look tired." I touch her face and hate when she flinches, but she catches herself quickly.

"Why don't you make mam and dad something to eat? I'm just going to get Scarlett settled."

I don't look to my parents to see what they are thinking. I've always been weird to them. So this behavior isn't anything new.

"Okay." Gage surprises me when he agrees. I wrap my fingers around Scarlett's hands.

"Well, goodnight, sweetheart." My mam sounds genuinely happy as she speaks to Scarlett.

"It was lovely meeting you all."

"We will catch up properly tomorrow." My mam promises as I leave the room with Scarlett.

"I look forward to it." Scarlett calls over her shoulder.

"Why are you being rude?" Scarlett asks the minute we are out of earshot. I don't answer her as I walk her to the bedroom. Once she's inside, I release her hand.

"You like Gage?" I take a step towards her.

"What?" She reaches up and touches her neck. I don't want her reaching for the pendant. I am here. She can reach for me, not take comfort in a ghost.

I fold my arms across my chest. I don't want to hurt her. "Why were you looking at him like that?"

Jealousy boils through me. I glance away as the emotion rides high inside me.

"He's nice to me. He tried to rescue me."

"What? From me?" I fire back.

Scarlett takes a step back, her brows drawing down. "Well, yeah." She sounds confused and I unfold my arms. There was a moment, when I introduced her, that I felt ten feet tall. I have a girlfriend, one who gets to meet my parents. The approval in my mam's eyes is new to me. Even with my dad, I can see how happy it makes him. It's different from the constant disappointment that I bring upon them.

"Dean." Scarlett's soft word has me glancing up at her, and I hate how her presence in my home is felt so strongly. What if she wasn't here? That thought has anger boiling my blood, and I don't want to feel that right now. I clear the space between us and grab her face, slamming my lips on hers, she doesn't respond and my kisses turn more brutal. Her hands smack into my chest and I stumble away from her.

Angry ocean eyes glare up at me, and I don't stop as I reclaim her face and steal another kiss. This time when she pushes me away, I don't release her and she kisses me back. We are moving until her back collides with the wall. She bites me and I release her.

"Jesus Christ, Scarlett." I lick blood off my lip. She has re-opened a recent cut.

I turn as she tries to walk away and I carry her to the bed. She kicks out, and when I pin her down, she's ready to scream. I clamp a hand over her mouth. My lips burn.

"What are you doing?"

She wriggles under me, her eyes burn with anger. I move my hand.

"I don't get it. I'm doing everything you want, yet it's not enough. What do you want from me?!" She's breathing heavily and I don't want to answer her question.

"I don't like how you are looking at Gage." I move my face closer to hers. Her gaze flickers to my lips.

"What? I can't make eye contact with your brother?"

I release her arms from above her head and sit back. The answer to that question is yes. I don't fucking want her making eye contact with Gage, but that sounds too many kinds of fucked up.

She hasn't moved, and once again, I don't want to look at all the feelings that are swirling around inside me. I lean over her and press a gentler kiss to her lips, but it's not enough.

I slip my tongue into her mouth and it's like something switches on inside her and she meets my kiss with a harshness I didn't expect from her.

CHAPTER TWENTY-FOUR

SCARLETT

A nger isn't even close to what I feel. Dean presses his cock against me. His hands roam my body possessively and I have no idea how to win with him. I slam my hands into his chest again and he leans back. Fresh blood wells up on his lip, I don't want him to stop, but I want to hurt him as much as he is hurting me.

He glares at me and I push him again. His lips find mine and I wriggle out from under him. I don't want this to stop, but anger has me breaking our kisses, while my body wants Dean's touch so much, no matter how rough it is. He drags me back and a part of me is elated as he pulls my top off before kissing me again. I grab the hem of his top and he quickly breaks the kisses and removes it before reclaiming me. My hands roam his wide shoulders before I dig my nails purposely into his back. He hesitates. I'm airborne and find myself smacked into the mattress with Dean over me.

"What are you doing?" His angry words make me wetter.

I have no idea what I am doing. Playing with fire? I am exhausted emotionally and I don't care right now. He doesn't wait for me to respond. He drags my trousers off me roughly and I kick out, connecting with his shoulder.

"Scarlett." My name is growled in a warning and he's removing his own trousers. His large erection springs free. He parts my legs roughly and moves himself into position.

"Get off me," I say, not meaning it at all.

I want to laugh or cry or scream. I could scream that he kidnapped me. I could do a lot of things, but instead I'm dragging him down to me and he pushes fully inside me in one swift movement. I don't cry out. I'm aware of his family in the living space. He moves over me and I moan into his neck, my sounds muffled. I push him again and he stops fucking me, his eyes dazed.

"Get off me," I repeat. He pulls out of me and I move out from under him. When he rolls onto his back I climb on top of him, and ride his hard cock with all the anger that boils through me. His hands grip my hips and I pull them off. His jaw clenches, but his enjoyment takes over as I ride him faster. He's perfect under me and I hate him all the more. His hands return to my hips, but fall away as my hand connects with his face. He's glaring at me in confusion, and I'm so close to cumming as I ride his cock hard. I explode over him and lean down, burying my face in his neck as I cry out my release. He jerks up into me and pounds until his cum sprays the walls of my pussy. I'm panting and so is he. I lean back so I can look into his dark eyes.

"What the fuck was that?" He asks and I have no answer for him, because I don't know myself.

I'm angry because I got to meet his family like this is real, and for a moment I wanted it to be real. But it isn't. I'm still looking down at him and bile starts to rise up my throat with the realization that I'm falling in love with Dean. I climb off him quickly and he sits up, staring at me.

"Scarlett?" He's holding up his hands. "You wanted that, too?"

I am falling in love with him—with the idea of us. I try to climb off the bed, but his hands circle my waist and he pulls me back.

"Scarlett. I didn't force you." His face looks panicked.

I try to push everything else down. "No, you didn't." I admit, I had wanted that even more than he did. He thinks that's why I'm trying to get away from him. His large hand touches my face and I feel it all the way down to my stupid toes. I close my eyes, unable to keep the flood of emotions hidden from him.

"You're crazy." His words brush my face. It doesn't sound like an accusation but a statement, one that doesn't seem to really bother him.

I pull away from his touch. "You're an asshole." I spit back.

He grins and gets off the bed and I'm ready to ask him, what are we doing? What is this between us? It is so much more now, but I still have no idea where I stand with him. My heart pounds faster in my chest.

I want to ask him how he feels, but I know how stupid that is. He drags on his trousers.

"You did good back there," he says, turning to me with his shirt in his hand. I drag my knees up to my chin. His gaze touches all over my skin. "It's only for two days." He finishes as he drags on his shirt.

Two days and then what? I don't answer him and he crawls back onto the bed.

"What are you thinking?" His gaze roams across my face like the answers might be there. I let my eyelids flutter closed and he grips my chin painfully, making me look up at him before I hit his hands away.

"Why won't you answer me?"

I feed off his anger. "I'm saving the happy Scarlett for your parents. Are they even your real parents?" I ask, and he flinches.

"No." His answer shocks me.

"I was adopted. So was Gage."

My chest tightens. "I didn't mean..." I start, but he climbs off the bed.

"I know we don't look alike. It was a fair assumption."

I hadn't even looked to see a resemblance; it was just that Dean could be lying to me.

He glances at me with a clenched jaw. I know better than to keep prodding him.

"What happened to your dad? It looks like someone beat him?" I try to reach for softer ground, but with Dean, there is none.

"Get some rest." He tells me, as he picks up his military boots. He pauses at the door and glances back at me. I don't know what I see in his dark eyes, but he shuts me off and leaves the room.

I want to go after him. I don't want to be alone. My fingers touch my pendant, but I don't find the same solace in it as I once did. It's like the day that Dean pulled it from my neck, it lost its magical ability to make me believe that everything would be okay. With Dean, I always feel like I'm crawling on my knees. I have no idea what I am feeling or what I am meant to feel. I lie back on the bed and drag the blanket over my naked body. I don't know what I wait for, but my mind is a jumbled mess as I fall asleep.

I wake and know it's morning, or close to morning time. Dean isn't beside me and I reach across and touch his side of the bed. It's cold and I don't remember him coming back to me last night. I roll onto my back and stare up at the ceiling. I can hear the soft chatter of voices and it sends my stomach spinning.

They seemed so normal. They appear like really nice people. So why don't I just run out there and tell them I've been kept here against my will? Why am I pretending? I roll onto my stomach. I know why, because a part of me wants to see what it would feel like to belong to him. When he introduced me to them, a thousand dreams came to life right there in his living space.

I have a family, I have a home, food on my table, and I have Dean—it was all so perfect that I thought I was going to fall down and sleep. It was like all the tightness that had held me upright just vanished from my body.

The handle of the door pushes down and I push everything aside with the thoughts of his dark eyes on me. I clutch the blanket and drag it tighter to my body. It isn't Dean. It's Gage. I'm ready to scream, maybe he sees the fear in me.

"I'm not going to hurt you. I'm going to help you."

He takes a step closer and I move deeper into the bed.

"Scarlett, I can get you out of here." His words are said with a smile and I let it sink in for one crazy second. He can help me leave, and go where?

"Get out." I can't hold his gaze and when he doesn't move, I look back up at him.

His confusion drags down his brows. "You want to stay here?"

"No." I blurt out. I don't. Not like this. It should never be like this. "He won't let you take me." I hold my head higher.

"If I found a way, would you come?"

The question is so heavy and I tighten my hold even further on the blanket. Tears blur my vision and I have no understanding of why.

"Yes," I whisper.

It's all he needs. He nods his head. "I'll find a way." He leaves me and I feel like I've betrayed Dean, which is crazy since he took me.

"He took you," I say out loud, reminding myself why I need to leave.

CHAPTER TWENTY – FIVE

DEAN

I'm staring into the sink. I feel sick.

"What's troubling you?" My mam reaches up and touches my cheek. I take my hands out of the water.

"Nothing. I'm just glad you are here." I tell her and she smiles up at me.

"You've always found it hard to talk about your emotions."

I look away from her. "Where's Gage?" I ask, glancing around the space. Dad is snoozing on the couch. Gage returns into the living space.

"Where were you?" I ask him and move away from the sink, wiping my wet hands on my jeans.

"Toilet." He fucking lies and I'm moving past him.

"She's fine." He speaks to me as I pass him. My heart beats too fast as I enter our room and she's pulling a t-shirt on. I get a peek of her smooth skin before it's covered up. Guilt shines in her eyes and I squeeze my eyes shut as an image of her with Gage claws its way into my mind.

"Dean?" She's standing in front of me when I open my eyes. Ocean eyes search my face for the reason of my distress. "Are you okay?" What a fucking question. No! I'm burning up with the thoughts of my brother even looking at you.

"Yeah, I was just seeing if you were hungry." I step in and place a kiss on her lips. She seems startled but kisses me back. Her soft hair falls through my fingers.

She's mine.

"What will I cook you?"

Her eyes widen. "I like pancakes." She bites her lip and a smile teases her mouth.

I'm mirroring her smile. "I can make pancakes with bacon."

"No bacon." Her smile widens and I steal another kiss.

"Maybe we can skip the food."

Her smile wavers, but she doesn't say no. She looks better this morning. The sleep has done her good. I need to feed her.

I entwine our fingers together and start walking towards the door, but before I reach it, she stops me.

"I need to wash my face."

Her face is perfect, she looks stunning in the mornings. I give her another kiss.

"Okay. I'll get started on your pancakes."

She tries to hide another smile, but fails, and I love it. I'm looking into ocean eyes realizing she's really sunk her nails into me—and I don't ever want her to let go.

"What do I smell?" My dad asks, rousing from the couch as I flip another pancake. Scarlett sits at the table where she always sits, but she's not relaxed like she normally is. Gage is sitting across from her and he keeps looking at her.

My mother works by my side, cutting up strawberries and making the tea.

She pauses and I look at her. She's smiling, "This is nice," she tells me before turning to the table where dad joins Gage and Scarlett. "This is nice," she repeats as she starts to set the table. For years she has tried to get us together and finally here we are, in a bunker with a girl I kidnapped. Yeah, it is perfect. I carry over the pancakes and enjoy how Scarlett keeps track of me. I serve her first. My mother is ready with the icing sugar that she sprinkles on before dropping some strawberries. I reach across and rearrange them.

Standing back, I serve Gage by slapping two pancakes onto his plate, one of them hangs off the edge and he pushes it back on, exhaling loudly. I finish mam's and dad's before placing two pancakes on a plate beside Scarlett. She's still watching me and I see the color in her cheeks. I leave the pan in the sink and sit down.

The smiley face I made with the strawberries, still sits untouched on Scarlett's plate.

"Eat," I say to her gently.

Her brows draw down and her eyes waver, but she starts to eat. My mam smiles at me and we all start to eat.

"This is really nice." My mam is beaming and I feel like shit.

"Why don't you tell us about your work?" Dad asks me across the table.

"Oh, Frank." My mam gives out.

My dad raises his fork, cutting her off. "We were attacked in our home because of his work. These men weren't government men, they were gangsters."

"Frank, please. Scarlett doesn't need to hear this." My mam protests again.

My mam tries to intervene again and I touch her hand. "Dad has every right to question me." I scratch my brow before cutting up my pancake. "The work I do for the government has me sometimes going undercover with dangerous people."

"Gage told us not to report the attack," Dad says.

"Gage was wrong." I speak while staring at Gage. "I can't get involved, but you could have reported the crime."

"You're telling me a lot, but nothing, really," Dad says.

I can nearly hear my mother say, 'Frank'.

"I'm telling you all I can tell you."

Dad points his fork at Scarlett. "Does she know what you do?"

I grin and it's not one bit fucking funny. I glance at Scarlett. "Yeah," I say. While looking at her, she does the oddest thing. She reaches across the table and touches my hand.

I have no idea what that means, but her touch is nice.

"Do you have family?" My mam asks Scarlett, thinking she is going to nice ground, but she isn't.

"My parents have passed." Scarlett answers and straight away she touches the pendant. I notice she has eaten her pancakes. I pick up one of mine and place it on her plate.

"I'm okay." She waves me off, but I grab some icing sugar and sprinkle it for her. Picking up the last slice of strawberry, I sit it in the center.

She hasn't taken her eyes off me. "Eat." She cuts it up and places a large piece in her mouth. I could watch her all day. When I glance back, Gage and dad are watching me.

"What?" I bark.

"Nothing." Dad's trying to hide a smile, while Gage looks ready to throttle me. I grin at him before patting mam's hand that rests on the table.

"Are you okay?" I ask her.

"I'm so happy to be here with you." She touches my face again and I see the love she has for me. She showers Gage with the same. She's a good mother. I kiss the inside of her hand.

"Have you any siblings?" My mam asks Scarlett.

"No. It was mostly just me and my dad. He died from cancer." She frowns and reaches for her pendant, but stops herself this time.

"I'm so sorry. What a horrible disease."

"Yeah, but he was a good father. So I have a lot of happy memories with him."

"What age where you?" My mam asks, and I'm ready to tell her to stop the interrogation, but Scarlett answers.

"Ten." She bites her lip.

"So young."

"What age was Dean when you adopted him?"

Gage drops his mug at her question and his gaze shoots to me. I'm not surprised. I've never mentioned us being adopted to anyone in my life. I never spoke of it. It isn't a big deal to me. But it is to my family.

Gage starts mopping up his tea.

"He was three months old. Gage was two." My mam sounds rattled.

I turn to Scarlett, wondering why she's brought this up. Her face is soft and I see there is nothing malicious in her words, but I'm still fucking stunned.

"Three months." Scarlett repeats, her eyes flickering to me before returning to my mam. "He's so lucky to have you."

"You have to keep her." My mam tells me.

My dad chuckles. "You found her weakness." My dad smiles at Scarlett.

"You told her we were adopted?" Gage's stunned voice pulls all the smiles off everyone's face.

"Yes."

"I've tried to talk to you for fucking years about it."

"Language." My mam reprimands Gage who apologizes but still doesn't drop it.

"And what? All of a sudden you decide to open up?" Gage tightens his hold on his fork.

I grin at him. "Yes."

Scarlett's ready to intervene, but I cut her a warning look and she sits back in her chair.

"Your brother has every right to tell who he wishes." My mam leans across the table towards Gage. He softens instantly when he looks at her. Dad is smiling like this is somehow funny.

"How about that song?" My dad asks Scarlett.

Her cheeks redden and she looks at me.

"If you don't want to, you don't have to," I say.

She relaxes. "Maybe later." She smiles sweetly at my dad and he accepts it.

"I need fresh air." My mam drags out her chair.

"Mam, that's not wise." I start and she waves me off.

"I'm not going alone, silly. Scarlett, what about we girls go for a walk?"

Both me and Gage say no at the same time.

My mam ignores me. "Come on, Scarlett."

Scarlett gets up and I hate what I see in her eyes. Hope. She's going to try to run.

"Scarlett doesn't want to, Mam," I say standing too, and gathering up the plates.

"Scarlett can speak for herself."

When I glance at my mam, she frowns at me.

"Why don't I go with you," Gage says to mam.

Both me and mam say no at the same time. The thoughts of Gage with Scarlett has me tightening my hold on the plates.

"You boys must think I'm going to eat her."

My dad leaves and returns with my mam's coat that she slips into.

"Now be a good boy, Dean, and open the door."

I'm staring at Scarlett. She hasn't tried to worm her way out of this and she won't look at me.

"Yeah, just let me get Scarlett's jacket." I leave the plates on the table and walk down to the bedroom. I pick up her army green jacket.

"Scarlett," I call her, and a few seconds later she appears in the doorway, but she won't step into the room. Her gaze flickers to the jacket before they return to my eyes.

"She's old, and she would never understand this."

Scarlett doesn't move, but I see the pulse in her neck beat rapidly.

"For her, please just go for the walk and come back."

She nods and I don't believe her.

I step up to Scarlett and she leans back so she can look at me. Fear that I've never felt before, clutches my chest. Fear of losing her. Fear of her not wanting to be with me.

"I don't want you to leave." I admit.

She still hasn't spoken, and that's scaring me.

"Scarlett." My mam calls down the hallway.

Scarlett looks over her shoulder before turning back to me with conflict in her ocean eyes. She's not listening to me.

"If you run. I will find you and I won't be happy." I threaten her and she bristles. I can see it was the wrong decision. She yanks the green jacket from my arms.

"Scarlett." I stop her from leaving and exhale loudly. "Please, don't run."

Her chest rises and falls quickly.

"Are you ready?" My mam appears and I release Scarlett's arm and she slips into the army green jacket.

"Yeah." Scarlett's voice is soft and my mam smiles at her. I hate each second of this. As I enter the kitchen, Gage stares at me and I shake my head at him. Just stay where you fucking are.

I look over my shoulder and my mam is smiling up at Scarlett who is staring at the keypad. I block her view and punch in the number. The door opens.

"The perimeter is alarmed. Don't go beyond the tree line." I tell them, as mam passes me. Scarlett helps her up the stairs avoiding my eyes completely. I stay at the bottom as they disappear.

"You want to tell me what's going on now, son?" My dad is behind me and I still cling to the door, unable to close it. Gage steps up to it and I quickly close the door, not letting him out.

"I need fresh air. Anyway, dad wants to talk to you."

DARKEST

I ignore Gage and walk away from the door.

"Son?" My dad is asking me for honesty.

"I'm a sniper," I say, and Gage curses.

CHAPTER TWENTY-SIX

SCARLETT

My heart is ready to explode from my chest. I'm outside without Dean. His mother is tiny beside me, her arm links with mine as we walk through the grass. A bird screeches overhead and I watch it fly away.

"My son is very taken with you." My attention snaps to Dean's mother. Oh, she has no idea. I smile at her.

"He struggled in school. He struggled his whole life with connecting with people. So it's wonderful to see the connection he has with you."

I can't look at her. I'm too taken with the green fields. I know beyond the hedge line is another field and then a road. It's freedom.

I notice Dean's mother is silent.

"The pendant around your neck?" She questions.

I touch it. "My father gave it to me."

"You touch it a lot." She smiles softly.

"It used to make me feel better." I ramble as I glare out at the hedge line. What the hell am I waiting for?

"Used to?" We've stopped walking and I glance down at Dean's mother.

I don't know how to answer her. It doesn't hold the same power anymore. My stomach tightens and I stare back at the house, knowing I'm wasting time.

"What's troubling you?" Dean's mother asks. "I know I'm the mother-in-law, but I'm a good listener."

I can't begin to imagine telling her the truth. There is something so innocent about Dean's mother. She has such a kindness about her. The fact she adopted two children speaks of her character. I'm also very aware of how she said mother-in-law.

I exhale loudly and she tightens her hold on my arm as we continue to walk.

"I just hate how the lines are blurring and I don't know what to make of it. I've always seen everything as black and white…" I drop off knowing I'm not making sense to her, but it's nice to talk out loud.

"Life isn't black and white, it's filled with colors," she says.

"More like shades of gray." I retort.

She laughs gently. "That too, but without the gray's and the colors, what would this life be?" She shrugs. "Not a place I'd like to live."

Where would I be today if Dean hadn't taken me? Would I still be stealing, or worse—dead? Would I have returned to my uncle? I shiver and tighten my hold on the little lady at my side.

"Me neither," I say out loud and she pats my hand.

We walk around the perimeter and I get to listen to all the stories about Dean and Gage when they were children. Dean sounds like he has some condition that wouldn't have been diagnosed back then. His mother was right, he really suffered with his emotions. He wasn't aware of them. He sounded numb, even as a child. I'm picturing a small Dean with his dark eyes. My stomach twists.

"He was never bullied, but he always kept to himself. Enjoyed his own company. He loved hunting." My stomach tightens at that. She has no idea. "I'm glad he found you."

I smile down at her and refocus on the surrounding landscape. I am wasting far too much time. How long have we been out here? He said if we walk past the tree lines, an alarm would go off. We walk close to the tree line and I pause. My heart hammers.

I release Dean's mother and so much swells in me. I need to leave. He took me. I step closer.

"Are you okay?" His mother's words bring me back, but it's not enough. I step out into the trees and nothing happens. I wonder if the alarm is screeching inside. I smile at the idea of his face.

"I'm fine." I step back out of the tree line and re-link my arm with Dean's mother.

"It's getting cold." She looks uncertain and walks with me back to the house.

Dean appears out of the house with Gage heavy on his heels. The moment he spots me, he stops running and he's frozen, staring at me. I see relief swim in his dark eyes. A matching pair of eyes behind him hold confusion and I don't blame Gage, but I wasn't about to leave his mother out here alone with a million questions. That's the excuse I tell myself anyway.

"I told you I wouldn't eat her." Dean's mother says the moment we reach a stunned Dean.

"The alarm went off." He's speaking to me.

"Sorry. I thought I saw something in the trees. I just went to investigate."

He nods his head, but his focus is still on my face, like he can't believe I'm still here. I wasn't sure if that made me stupid.

"You look cold, Mam." Gage steps forward and takes his mother's hand and she releases me. Gage won't meet my eyes and I stuff my hands into my pockets.

"Nothing a hot cup of tea won't fix." Dean's mother climbs the steps and I don't. Dean stands close to them in a t-shirt. He has to be getting cold, but he stares out towards the forest.

"What did you think you saw?" He asks me once Gage and his mother are gone.

I shrug. *Freedom*. "A bird."

"You want me to kill it."

I'm ready to give up, but he's grinning and I find my lip tugging up. "No, I don't want you to kill anything." Ever again, I don't add, but it's what I'm thinking.

"Thank you." He clears the space between us and places a kiss on my lips.

"For what?" I ask.

"For not running."

I let out a short laugh. "I was hardly going to leave your mother here alone with a million questions." I can't look at him because I can't let him see the truth. That I love him, and I don't want to leave. I glance back out at the forest and reach up, unclipping my pendant. It feels so light in my hands. Dean's watching me.

"I used to think that when I touched the pendant that it made everything okay."

"There's nothing wrong with that, Scarlett." Dean's words are soft.

"I know. But it made me turn a blind eye to everything that hurt me." I frown and tighten my hold on the chain. "Since you, I've had to face all my wounds." In the most savage way, but I leave that part out.

"Great." Dean folds his arms across his chest.

"It's not a good thing. I can't keep burying my head in the sand. My dad is gone and he's not coming back." I give a short laugh that hurts my heart, but it's the truth. I walk away from the house and Dean follows at a distance. I keep walking until I hit the tree line again. I could run if I wanted to, but I know I don't want to.

I stop when the soil doesn't look so hard and kneel down, digging a small hole. I hold the pendant, and Dean kneels down beside me. His presence makes me stronger and I drop the pendant into the hole. A part of me doesn't want to let it go, but since I was ten, I've been reaching for it like an addict. At ten I couldn't understand him leaving, but now, now I understand it wasn't a choice. It's the only thing in life that isn't a choice. It comes to us all.

Tears drip off my chin and I wipe them with the back of my hand before pushing the clay over the small hole. I let some damaged part of me go, too. Dean pulls me into him without warning and I'm crying. I'm crying for the loss of my father. The ten-year-old in me finally lets it out.

I'm raw, but I've never felt so alive when Dean and I return to the house. Gage watches my every move and his eyes hold such judgment. Dean entwines our fingers and I hold on to his hand tighter as we step into the living space. His parents are watching TV. They acknowledge us with smiles.

"Gage is cooking dinner for us," Dean says.

Gage gets up out of his chair. "The final meal," he says.

Dean's hand tightens around mine. "What does he mean?" I ask as quietly as I can. Dean doesn't answer but leads me out of the living space and into the small bathroom. He closes the lid of the toilet and makes me sit down. I do, and watch as he runs a face cloth under the tap. He returns to me.

"You have some mud on your face." He explains before he starts to clean me. I can't keep looking into his dark eyes. All I can think of is who would clean my face if I was still living on the streets? No one.

I bite the inside of my jaw and try to ease the tidal wave of emotions that want to pour out. "Thank you, Dean."

He pauses cleaning my face. "Why didn't you run?"

My stomach trembles. "I already told you." My voice is as weak as my lie. "Do you want me to leave?" I ask, frowning.

His smile is quick. "Why don't you tell me why you didn't run?" His hands rest on my thighs now and I feel the heat through my jeans.

"I didn't want to." My heart threatens to burst from my chest as blood roars in my ears.

"Why?" He hasn't blinked.

It is wrong what I am feeling. I know that. "Where would I go?"

He flinches, and I hate the lie that he swallows easily. He finishes cleaning my face before rising. "I'm happy you are still here, Scarlett, even if you're not." He leaves the bathroom. How is it that I feel like a horrible person for not being truthful? But the truth is too much right now.

I'm raw for the rest of the day, but something heavy has been lifted off my chest. I sit with Dean's parents and watch TV. I have moments when I glance at them and feel like laughing. I'm sitting in between two seventy-year-olds in a bunker. It's crazy, but nice.

Gage cooks, and each time I look at him, he catches my eye and I quickly turn away. Dean leaves and he takes his long bag with him. I know it's his gun and I hate the worry that gnaws at my stomach. My thoughts are more disturbing—I just hope whatever he's doing—that he stays safe and doesn't get caught. What kind of person does that make me?

Time moves slowly and when Dean returns, it's dinner time. He doesn't come back in with the bag, but when his eyes meet mine, his flash with something I don't understand.

"Can I have a word?" I ask as nicely as possible as I bury the urgency that threatens to strangle me.

"Yeah." He nods and holds out his arm for me to walk first. When I pass him, he catches my hand and entwines our fingers together. I look down at our joined hands and we walk to the bedroom.

"Don't be long, the food is ready." Gage's voice is rough.

"Ignore him." Dean tugs me and I look up into his smiling face.

"Where were you?" I ask the moment we step into the bedroom. Dean releases my hand.

"I had something to take care of."

"What?" I ask and dread curls its thin fingers around my spine.

"I think it's best you don't know what I just did."

Bile crawls up my throat. "Don't tell me." I blurt, but I need to know. "Did you kill someone?"

Dean tilts his head like I'm naïve, before walking away from me. "Did you kill someone?" I ask again and follow him. "I can't be with a killer, Dean."

He stops and spins around. "Be with?"

I point between us as my heart rate escalates. "This thing with us." I'm losing the ability to speak as Dean takes a step towards me and folds his arms across his chest.

"Explain it to me."

Now he is being an asshole. I'm ready to walk away and maybe he senses it.

"What I did, I had to do."

I bite my jaw and my hand reaches for my pendant but falls away. "Like with the jogger?"

"No." Dean answers quickly and truthfully.

I have no idea what he did; if he had killed someone or not.

"I can be honest with you, Scarlett, but I don't want you to leave."

So, I'd leave if I knew the truth?

"I don't want to leave, either." I admit.

"Because you have nowhere to go," Dean says.

I shake my head. "No. Because I like being here with you." My heart races as the truth pours out.

He clears the space between us and takes my face in his hands. His kiss is almost panicked and I shiver into it. "Even if I wanted to, I would never let you go."

I push him away from me. "What? You can't just say something like that." I tighten my fists.

"It's the truth." He doesn't seem fazed at all by what he just said.

"Don't you want to know how I really feel?" I ask.

"Yes. I actually do." He folds his arms across his wide chest as he waits for his answer.

"You will only ever know if you let me go and I come back here out of my own free will, Dean. Otherwise, you will never really know."

CHAPTER TWENTY-SEVEN

DEAN

Let her go? That isn't going to happen, not even if it proves she wanted to be here. Because I'm not taking the risk. Just like when she went outside with my mother. She never had a chance. The alarm went off the moment she stepped outside the tree line.

My father laughed when I told him I'm a sniper. It felt good telling him the truth, even if he didn't believe me. I laughed along with him and that ended my so-called joke.

The meal that Gage makes is nice. Scarlett is quiet, but she isn't exactly a talker either. When my mam speaks to her, her whole face softens and she is stunning. All I want to do is take her down to the room and kiss every inch of her perfect body. She is avoiding meeting my eye and I get that. She's still mad at me. I'm not proud of keeping her here against her will. A part of me wants to let her go just to see if she will come back.

I want to tell her where I was and what I did. A part of me wants to see her smile, but another fears what she will say. I'd taken the piece of paper that she had written her name and address down on and tracked down her uncle. It was the first time I took a life for no other reason than pleasure. I would have preferred to make it slow, but I didn't have time on my side, and since she told me he abused her, each night it's all I've wanted to do. I'm glad he can never hurt her again.

"Are you ready for tomorrow?" Gage interrupts my thoughts.

I put down the knife and fork. "Yeah."

"What's tomorrow?" Fear fills Scarlett's eyes.

"I have a meeting," I say.

"With the government?" My mam asks and she looks shifty too.

"Yeah, Mam."

I glance at Gage. What the fuck is he playing at, mentioning tomorrow in front of everyone?

"Are you coming with me?"

"I'll stay here and hold the fort." I want to smack him in the face. Like fuck he will. He's pushing me too far.

"I'll need back up in case things go south."

"Why would things go south?" The worry that laces Scarlett's words has me wanting to grin at Gage.

"It's only a meeting," I say, and she frowns at me.

"Is this with the people that attacked me and your father?" My mam sounds worried, and now I'm ready to drag Gage across the table. It's one thing to annoy me, but to worry her is unacceptable.

"Mam, I'll be with him." Gage tells her and I see her small shoulders relax. This time I do grin at Gage. If I'm going down, he's coming with me.

Mam and Scarlett clean up.

"You know they are going to clip me," I say to Gage as he follows me to the gun room. Dad is back to watching TV. He never was one for hovering around us. I used to think that maybe mam wanted us more than he did, but with time, I understood this is just his way.

"He wants to talk to you. You're meeting at the warehouse where you shot the woman." Gage glares at me like he has a right to judge me. I take three guns off the wall.

"She was going to shoot my client." I defend myself and Gage shakes his head in disgust. Right now, I regret that split second decision. I should have let her kill Damien. I would still have my money, and I wouldn't be in this fucking mess.

"It's Rian Steele," Gage says and I stop pulling guns off the wall.

"You're only telling me this now?" The son of Cillian Steele. A gang who controls all the south.

"I only found out. You apparently killed a relation of theirs."

I close my eyes and try to think of a way out of this. There is none. This is the worst possible outcome that I could imagine—bringing Rian Steele down on my head.

"He's going to clip me." I repeat. "He doesn't want fifty G's. He wipes his ass with that kind of money."

"He said he just wants to talk."

Gage knows full well that this isn't going to be a talk.

We fall into a silence as I continue to take guns off the wall. I stop at five, knowing I'm not going to shoot Rian Steele, even if the opportunity presents itself. I also know my family will never be safe, even this bunker won't keep him from finding us if he wants to. I've really fucked up this time.

"Let the girl go," Gage says finally.

I glare at him. "No."

"Christ, Dean, you know this is wrong."

"She could have run today, but she didn't."

Gage steps up to me. "Running isn't the fucking same as letting her go."

I grab his collar and push him away from me. "I'm not letting her go." He can fuck right off. I throw the guns into a bag and leave the gun room. Stowing them in the bedroom, I sit on the bed and run my hands across the top of my head.

The door opens and I'm ready to tell Gage I've had enough of him, but ocean eyes take me in.

"Hi." She pulls down the sleeves of her white top over her hands. "Are you okay?" Her concern draws down her brows. Her lips look red and swollen and I haven't even kissed her yet. It's from her constant chewing on them.

"Yeah." I answer and she steps closer to me. She reaches for her neck but stops herself before sitting down beside me.

"Is something bad going to happen?"

I glance at her. "No."

She gnaws on her lip and I hate it. "Scarlett, nothing bad is going to happen." I lie.

Her smell encircles me, and right now, all I want to do is bury myself deep inside her. She pushes her hair behind her ears and surprises me when she stands up and pulls her top off. Her breasts bounce free and my cock grows hard instantly. She doesn't waver as she pushes down her jeans and underpants.

Fuck me!

Her skin is soft in my hands as I grab her hips and guide her to me. She straddles me and I've never seen anything so beautiful. Her cheeks darken as she tucks more hair behind her ears. Bending her head, she kisses me and straight away I know this is different. I meet her gentle kiss, my cock throbs inside my own jeans and I hold back from grabbing her and placing her under me. Her hands tug on my beard as she pulls my face closer to hers and deepens the kiss by pushing her tongue into my mouth. She tastes of mint. I smile into her kiss, noting she had brushed her teeth before coming in here. She must have had the intention of seducing me.

She grinds herself against my cock and I groan into her mouth. I lift her off me and push down my jeans, noting the wetness staining them from her pussy. My gaze glides up her perfect body as I pull off my t-shirt and remove my boxers. I sit back down on the bed. Her nipples are erect as her gaze roams across my cock before she climbs back up on me. I take a hard nipple in my mouth and suck. She groans as she shuffles forward, my cock at her opening. I hold back from slamming it into her and let her slowly and painfully move herself down on my cock. It's my turn to groan as the pleasure builds quickly. I release her nipple and take the other one in my mouth. Her hands clutch my shoulders as she continues to ride me slowly, but she's lifting the whole way up before moving back down. My cock is soaking with her wetness and I want to taste her. But I don't stop her as she continues to ride me. It's slow, and when I release her nipple, she leans away and her hands travel to my face. She pushes my head back and I'm staring into her ocean eyes. My stomach quivers with what I see there—love.

My cock twitches inside her and I grip her hips helping her move faster. I'm so close to cumming, that when she gets faster, her tits slap against my chest and I explode inside her. She continues to move up and down as she searches for her own release. I lift her off me and she cries out. I don't make her wait long before I lay her on her back and push my cock back inside her. My cum stains her inner thighs, and I start to push inside her. Gripping her legs, I spread them and push myself fully in.

"Dean." Her calling out my name makes me grow harder. I want her to empty her sweet juices all over me. I move down and hover over her. Her fingers reach up and grip the back of my head. She directs me to her lips and I kiss her like a dying man, because tomorrow I might be dead. I don't have much hope of coming back alive. I push my cock into her while keeping my lips locked with hers. She's panting against me and I keep moving faster. Her groans turn harsher and her lips seek out mine hungrily as I move faster, pumping myself into her pussy. She cries out into my neck as she finally reaches her high. I keep my pace, but slow down as her breathing fans out along my neck. Her lips press against my shoulder and neck before trailing up to my cheek, and when my gaze meets hers, I see the love there again. I want to tell her how I feel about her, but I also know now it isn't the time.

I pull out of her slowly, and move both of us up the bed, where I just hold her. She allows me to. We are both still breathing heavily and my cock grows hard with her in my arms. I don't think I could ever get used to Scarlett.

They say your first love cuts the deepest. Right now, I am pretty sure that she will leave a permanent scar on me if she ever leaves. Her name is very fitting.

I press a kiss to the top of her head and hold her closer. Her lips press against my arm that circles her chest and I wonder what she is thinking.

"4948," I say, and my heart thumps. Scarlett tries to turn in my arms, but I hold her firm.

"That's the code to the door." I can only hope she doesn't use it tonight, but right now, I know deep down that I won't stop her, because I love her.

CHAPTER TWENTY-EIGHT

SCARLETT

*T*he next morning I woke up to a piece of paper on the pillow next to me. I wasn't expecting a love letter, but what was scrawled across the page made my lips tug down and my temperature rise.

4948—the code, with his name scrawled at the bottom. That's it, but it's my freedom. Freedom that I'd take, no matter how hard it would be. I left that morning with tears burning my eyes and a sickening feeling in my heart.

"Did you see my pink top?"

I tuck my hair behind my ear and shake my head. I try not to talk to the other girls at the half-way house. They're full of questions, ones I refused to answer. Two weeks, it's been two weeks since I last saw Dean, and each morning I wake up with fear of him finding me, but also an unbelievable amount of excitement. He still hasn't come.

"Are you sure?"

I glance at my roommate again. "Yeah. I'm sure." She narrows her eyes and leaves the room as I get ready to do my duties in the kitchen. Every guy with a beard or dark eyes makes me think of Dean. Pancakes and banana sandwiches became his thing as well. I feel like I left a part of me back in the bunker. I didn't realize how much I healed while being there with him—not until I was no longer with him. My stomach tightens as I fasten the apron around my waist. His mother's small face makes me guilty every time I picture it. What did she think when they woke up to find me gone? What did Dean do when he arrived back to see me gone? Or Gage? I'm sure Gage was happy. I exhale loudly as I make my way to the kitchen. Taking a hair net off the wall before entering, I stuff all my hair into it. This wasn't the life I wanted, but at least it was my choice.

In the evenings, before curfew, I walk the streets and find myself searching for him in stranger's faces. I smile now when I think of his grin, before it burns my eyes and I take all that aggression and sadness out on the crockery like I do every single day.

This is what I wanted, freedom. It just doesn't taste as good as I expected. My stomach twists and turns when I think maybe, just maybe, I made a mistake. But then I pull my head out of the clouds. I was kidnapped. There was no other answer, but to escape when the opportunity arose. That's what normal people do.

You're not normal, Scarlett.

"Scarlett, you have a visitor." Everything in me freezes at those words, and it's a split second when I think it could be Dean, and my heart leaps into my throat.

"Me?" I question, trying to even out my breathing. My superior steps closer to me and the other girls go back to work.

"You know you don't have to do anything you don't want to. That's what we are here for." Her smile is gentle and it relaxes me. That's what the half-way house is for—the homeless, the women who run for countless reasons. Some are hiding here from abusive partners.

"It's okay." I wipe my hands on my apron and pull the hair net from my head as I follow my supervisor from the kitchen. Fear makes my knees wobbly and I want to veer off and find a spot to lie down in. The fear drains everything from me, including logic.

She steps aside and I lock my knees. I want to reach for something, but I hold still as Gage thanks my supervisor.

"This room has CCTV." She warns him.

"I won't be but a moment."

His voice makes me shiver. "What do you want?" I ask, my voice doesn't sound like my own.

He points at the small table and chairs to our left for visitors. I sit down, glad to get off my feet. I'm not sure how much longer my legs can hold me up.

"How are you?" Not a question I am expecting.

"I didn't tell anyone." I know that's what he really wants to ask.

His smile is instant. "I know. It's been two weeks, Scarlett."

I keep glancing at the door and my heart pounds too heavily against my chest. I rub the spot that hurts.

"He isn't here." Gage frowns and drops his eyes and something else grips me by the throat.

"Did something happen? Is he okay? Are your parents okay?"

"My parents are fine. My mother is wondering why you ran off, but they have other things to keep them occupied."

I don't want to know. I don't want to hear it. I know leaving was a mistake. I should never have left him. Maybe now I'll never get another chance with Dean.

"He's dead, isn't he?" I'm nodding as I look away from Gage. The clock on the wall ticks, it's five past eleven.

I bite my lip as my eyes and throat burn before looking back at Gage.

"He was shot." He confirms.

I lean in and cover my mouth with my hand.

"He isn't dead, Scarlett."

Salty liquid flows into my mouth.

"He's searching for you. That's what I'm doing here. Helping him."

I snivel and sit up straighter. I'm not sure how I feel about that.

Gage slips a piece of paper across the table. "Each day he gives me a piece of paper in case I find you. So this is today's."

I take it and open it slowly. It's his handwriting. My heart thumps. *Blackrock Beach, tomorrow morning. I'll be there waiting for you. Dean.*

"He goes there every day." Gage confirms and my eyes blur. I swallow and glance back up at his dark eyes.

"If you don't arrive, he'll stop searching, once he knows I have found you. He won't ever bother you again." Gage reaches across the table maybe to comfort me, but I pull away from his touch. It's not the touch I seek or want.

"You look good, Scarlett." He taps the table when I don't respond and gets up.

He's frowning down at me and his lips part like he has so much more he needs to say, but he closes his mouth and glances up at the camera. The buzz of the door has him pulling it open, and leaving, he doesn't look back. I blink and tears spill.

I return to the kitchen and try to turn down my emotions while I scrub pots and pans until my fingers are raw. Once my shift ends, I stay in my room. I normally take a walk through the city, but not today.

The room I sit in has two single beds and a double locker for the possessions we manage to get away with. I have seen so many battered women come and go in the last two weeks, that it makes me sick. Their wounds will slowly disappear, but inside they never really do. How many times have I heard that you have to confront your monsters in order to make them disappear? Too many times. I know I have to do it, but it doesn't make it any less terrifying. Dean isn't exactly a monster. I love him. But he took my freedom from me. He made me face all my demons head on, and he is the last one I need to face.

I leave the half-way house close to four in the morning. I take the night bus out as far as it will go and walk the last twenty minutes to the beach. The moment the smell of sea water hits me, my stomach tightens. The wind has picked up and I tighten my hold on my hand-me-down black jacket. Each time I've put it on, I've wondered who has worn it before. Did they find their happy ever after, or are they still angry and seething from the wrongs that were bestowed upon them?

I take the ten steps down until my feet hit the sand. Stopping, I look up and down the beach and it's empty. Taking off my shoes and socks, I let my feet sink into the sand. I carry my shoes as I walk towards the water, the waves crash across my feet and I close my eyes as the wind carries a drizzle of rain with it. I hold my hands out on either side of me and squeal as the water bashes up to my knees. The cold water is sharp and it's a reminder I'm alive right now, at this moment.

I can taste the salt on my lips as the sea continues to bash me. The next wave is bigger and forces me to run back when all I really want to do is run into the water. I open my eyes as my heart pounds.

I want to swim in the rain, I had told him once. It felt like such a long time ago. So much can change in two weeks.

"It's beautiful." His voice fills me with an overwhelming amount of sadness and the waves seem to respond with harshness against my legs.

"You're beautiful."

I can't turn around, I don't want to all of a sudden. I lean my head back and close my eyes.

"I didn't think you would leave."

His voice carries a note of his own heartache and it's closer to me, making me open my eyes.

"What do you want?" I say, and finally look to my left where he stands. His trousers are rolled up to his knees and the wine jumper he wears doesn't look very warm. Dark eyes search my face and my stomach squirms, so I glance away.

"I needed to make sure you were okay."

"Didn't Gage tell you I was fine?" I'm looking back out into the waves. "He said you got shot."

I glance at him again. "My shoulder." I notice how his arm is hanging limply at his side.

"Shouldn't you have it wrapped up?"

His grin sends butterflies floating through my system. It's a rush that makes my feet tingle.

"Are you worried?" He asks.

"No. Just hoping it's your trigger hand."

His laugh is loud and I find myself smiling too. "It actually is."

"Good."

His smile has me smiling, but when his vanishes, my body quivers as he takes a step towards me.

"I should have never given you that code." He's shaking his head.

Now, I want to leave. "You gave me my freedom."

"I lost you. I lost the only thing I have ever loved."

I bite my lip and look back out into the waves. "Don't say that." My nose burns with a rush of pain.

"It's true. I didn't think you would leave." His words end on a laugh, but it holds no humor.

Guilt weighs heavily on me. The drizzle in the air grows heavier. "I had to leave, Dean." I glance at him and he wavers before I blink. "If I didn't leave, I'd never really know." I swallow and look away from him. "What I feel is wrong. It's not natural."

He takes another step closer to me. "What do you feel?"

"Too much." I frown again. "You took me."

He runs a hand across his face. "I'm sorry."

I blink and tears fall. "Thank you."

He shakes his head and another wave hits my legs hard. "What are you thanking me for?"

"I'm so sick of wrongs being done to me and no one apologizing. No one has ever been held accountable for their actions," Salty tears fill my mouth. "So, thank you."

"We all have to meet our maker one day."

I'm ready to smile, I didn't peg Dean as religious, but when I glance at him, I see he is serious.

"Yeah, we all do."

"So, I'm trying to shave some of my wrongs off the list," he says before taking another step towards me. "I hope she's female and I can flirt my way into Heaven because the rest of the list is pretty long."

I'm laughing and it feels good.

"Build a life with me, Scarlett." Once again I'm ready to dismiss him. "Let me make it up to you. I want you to be my family." He reaches for me and I'm unsteady, his words undoing me. I want to belong. Isn't that what this life is all about? Belonging to people who love you.

His large hand is warm when it touches my face, and I sob with a smile at the contact. I've missed his touch, his smell.

"I love you." He's dipping his head trying to catch my eye and I believe him. "My mother is killing me over you leaving."

I laugh again through my pain.

His smile slowly dies. "Please tell me you'll give me one more try."

I think deep down, I knew I would search for him. He was the first person who ever saw me, and I'm proud of what I have become.

He doesn't raise his other arm and it reminds me he was shot. "You want to tell me what happened?"

"I promise I will, but I want something in return."

Is he seriously trying to bargain with me? The rain grows heavier and my legs are pretty cold at this stage. "What do you want?"

His gaze flickers to my lips, but he doesn't kiss me, or ask for a kiss as I thought that's what it would be, instead he takes my hand in his.

"Swim with me in the rain. You have a home now. A home with me."

More tears flow and I almost don't want him to see me like this. I can't answer him but tighten my fingers around his hand. "I'll swim with you."

His smile is wide and the darkness in his eyes eases up as he pulls me into him.

"You can't take it back," he warns.

I stand on the tips of my toes and press my lips to his. "I love you, Dean." I admit. I love the effect my words have on him. His eyes widen in disbelief and he reminds me of a child at this moment.

I'm screaming as I'm waist deep in the water. "I change my mind!" I scream as another wave lifts me. The rain is warmer than the ocean and this isn't how I imagined it.

"I won't let you drown." Dean pulls me to his chest.

"I'm sorry Dean, but I don't have the best confidence in you."

"Why?" He sounds so wounded.

"You only have one arm." I remind him.

With his one arm, he pulls me into him again. "I won't let anything hurt you again."

The rain soaks us and I wonder for the first time what we must look like from the road.

"Okay." I take his face in my hands and run them along his beard. The bristles tickle my palm. "Let's try this again. My name is Scarlett, and I'm a singer who has discovered I don't like swimming in the rain."

His laughter sends my heart racing. "I'm Dean. I'm unemployed right now. I recently packed in my last job, but don't worry, I have lots of money." His grin has me leaning in and placing a kiss on his lips. His hand worms its way around my waist and he lifts me along with the next wave and right here, in his arms—there is no other place I would rather be. I am exactly where I belong.

CHAPTER TWENTY-NINE

DEAN

Two weeks previously....

She looks like an angel as she sleeps. I don't want to leave. The note in my hand feels heavier than a gun. That's what it is. I'm handing her something that could destroy me. I place the note on the pillowcase, before placing a kiss on her forehead. She stirs, and I know I need to leave before she wakes up and starts asking me questions that I just can't answer right now.

I pick up the green army bag from the gunroom before entering the living room. Gage is drinking a cup of tea and nods at me over the rim before downing it like a drink.

"I'll drive."

I take a look around the space and wonder if I'll see it again. I'm not a martyr by any means, but the most important things to me are under this roof. I need to protect them.

"Let's go." I punch in the code and Gage pulls the door behind him. Once outside, I throw the bag into the back of the car.

"Do you need to give me the code for the door?" Gage asks while climbing in. He's refusing to meet my eye.

I snort. "Are you afraid that I will die today?" I ask.

"Yes." He turns and backs down the driveway.

"I gave the code to Scarlett."

I can feel his gaze on me, but I don't turn to meet his eye, and he doesn't say anymore, as we drive to what I feel is the wrong thing to do.

"He's going to clip me." I repeat for the hundredth time, I don't see this going any other way.

Gage smacks my chest. "Are you wearing a vest?"

"Yeah." His gaze meets mine, and I don't like the worry I see in his. "Then you're fine."

"So encouraging." I answer. We fall into a silence the rest of the drive.

I've never met Rian Steele in person, but I know of him. Ruthless and cold, that's what I've heard. He's never sought me out to do business with him, and I'm glad of that, but now, being dragged to him for shooting Kane's wife, I'm sick to my stomach. I should have let Damien die that day. I would be free of this shit.

The private airport's gates are open and we enter.

"You have the money?" Gage asks while driving into the only hanger that's open.

"Nah, I left it at home in the safe." My fingers drum along my leg. I'm fucking nervous, but I need to shut this shit down before it gets me killed. "Yeah, I have the money." I brought the fifty grand, although I know that's not what Rian Steele wants. He wants flesh, blood—he wants me.

"Is he coming alone?" I ask Gage while still staring out the window.

I want to get out and scan all the rooftops. All the places that a sniper could be. I reach in the back and grab the bag. Removing the guns, I stash two of them randomly around the car. The other three I put on me.

"You know he will search you?" Gage says.

I nod and my heart picks up as a car drives into the hanger. The black Bentley leaves no doubt of who the driver is.

"Think of mam and dad," Gage says, like he can see how much I want to fucking run.

"I'm here because of them." I answer.

He opens his door. "No, you're here because of her." He means Scarlett. I get out and drag the green army bag with me.

The door of the Bentley opens and Rian Steele steps out. A fag hangs from his mouth. He flicks it across the tarmac and blows smoke high into the air. Pushing his hair out of his eyes, he claps his hands. "Dean." He approaches me with a predatory look in his eyes. He grips my hand and pulls me into his chest. He's bigger than me, but I like to think I could hold my own against him. Yeah, he's an intimidating fucker, but I hope it doesn't show.

"Rian."

He scratches his jaw with his left hand, three of his fingers are clad with rings. It's his boxing hand; I wouldn't like to feel the power behind those fists, or the destruction those rings would cause. Maybe that's what the purpose of them are. His own weapon.

"Did you bring my money?" I throw the bag at his feet and he doesn't pick it up. He clicks his fingers, and one of the three men that are with him, comes forward and picks it up. Rian glances at Gage but doesn't acknowledge him.

"What does it feel like?" Rian asks.

"What?" I don't want to play games. I need to get back and make sure Scarlett doesn't use the code. That she doesn't leave me.

"To shoot an innocent woman." He holds his hands up and grins. "I mean... I've killed a lot of people, but, women aren't my thing."

I run my hand down my beard. "What do you want?" I fire back. Gage moves and Rian holds up two fingers, freezing him in place. I get to feel the power behind his fist. Blood splashes the tarmac as my head snaps back. The rings cut into my flesh and I hold my face for a moment before looking back up at Rian. He appears like he hasn't moved at all.

"What. Did. It. Feel. Like. To. Shoot. A. Woman?" He asks again.

I spit a mouthful of blood out on the tarmac. My jaw aches. "Nothing. It never feels like anything." I answer honestly. Tracking them was more fun than pulling the trigger.

"Who was the client that paid you?"

I'm shaking my head. It's my life's work on the line. "I'm not saying."

Rian throws his head back laughing before clapping his hands. I glance at Gage, who shakes his head. He doesn't get it. I can't give a client's name. If I do, I'll have every other fucker trying to clip me.

I turn to Rian and his fist collides with my jaw again. I hit the ground hard and this time I can't keep in the pain.

"You know I can't tell you. Everyone I've worked for would have a price on my head." I stand and wipe more blood from my mouth. His gun is in my face and I raise my hands slowly.

Jesus Christ, I knew he might try to clip me, but not like this. "I gave you your fifty grand," I say.

"It's not about the money. When one of our men wants blood for his relative, we deliver."

I didn't think someone like him would do the work for his men. I keep that to myself, not wanting a bullet between my eyes.

"What ever happened to that girl?" He asks.

"She escaped," I answered without blinking, thinking of her running across the field.

He nods. "What did she see?"

"I just wanted to fuck her." It was the partial truth and he buys it by taking the gun out of my face, or maybe he doesn't give a shit for what my reasons were for taking Scarlett.

"You will have to pay for the life you took. I'll have a few jobs for you."

I'm already shaking my head and the gun returns.

"This isn't a fucking debate. You will do these jobs or you die." He nods his head.

I want to disagree. The gun fires and it takes me a moment to feel the burn in my shoulder. I stumble back and sound ceases as my fingers come away coated in blood.

"How about now?" Rian's voice penetrates my shock.

I blink and Gage is beside me. He doesn't speak, but he's there.

I don't answer and he cocks the gun and points it at my leg. "Okay!" I shout. "Okay. Fine."

He puts the gun away and smiles. "I said I would shoot you and I did. So the debt is repaid. I'll be in touch, Dean."

He salutes me and I have a moment of relief before dizziness washes over me and I stumble to the ground.

Gage grabs me and pulls me up before leading me to the car. The drive moves in and out of focus until it finally grows dark.

I wake up the next morning in the hospital with my mam hovering over me. Gage is here too, and the moment I look at him he shakes his head. She's gone. My mam's questions confirm it. Scarlett ran the moment she got the chance. Can I really blame her? *No.*

I lie back into the pillows as my mother peppers me with questions. Who shot me? When did it happen? Where is Scarlett? Is everything okay? Why am I not speaking? Gage finally takes her from the room.

"You know she's worried," he says, filling me up a glass of water.

"I know, but right now I don't have answers for her." I pull the IV out of my arm and hiss.

"What are you doing?" Gage asks.

"I need to find her."

The door opens and a nurse arrives in. She takes one look at me and moves to my bed.

"Don't bother, I'm going." I stand up and hate the weakness in my limbs.

"You won't make it to the elevator." She warns.

"Watch me."

"He'll drag himself," Gage tells the nurse before he pushes me back onto the bed.

"You stupid motherfucker!" I roar with pain.

Gage laughs and the nurse demands he leaves as she hooks me back up to the IV. All I want to do is find Scarlett, but whatever she injects into the drip sends me into a sleep.

It takes a few days before I'm released. The moment I get out, I search for her on the streets. A part of me hopes I don't find her, while another craves her face, her ocean eyes. Gage surprises me by helping. We start early in the morning and don't stop until the night time falls. Every shelter dwindles my hope. There are six in the area and we split them up.

"Drink your soup." My mam warns me as I stare out the window at the rain. It reminds me of her. Rainy days make me sad now.

"I am, Mam." My mam pats my hand and returns to the stove. Dad sits on the couch with his head resting back as he snores. I don't want to be here, but my mam is happy to be taking care of me. She asks each day about Scarlett and I hate it. I have no answer. Gage arrives and I look at him. It's his eyes. I know it. He found her.

He sits down and mam places a bowl in front of him. "I gave it to her."

My heart leaps. He really found her. "I think she'll be there." His smile has hope blossoming inside me.

Gage told me the truth. She is here. Flesh and Bones. Right in front of me. Her hair is loose and wild, as the wind lifts the brown strands and throws them in every direction. She has her trousers rolled up, the waves crashing against her legs. There is peace in her stance. She has her arms outstretched like she is standing in front of something majestic. I glance out at the raging water and I suppose it is, but nothing is as powerful as Scarlett. I take off my boots and roll up my jeans. Each step makes me feel unworthy of her. The closer I get, the more I want to pause and watch her.

"It's beautiful," I say, and something in me breaks when she stiffens at my voice. I want to touch her. I want my Scarlett back.

"You're beautiful." I continue, and right now all I can think of is, I found her. I found Scarlett amongst the waves—and this time, I will never let her go.

THE END

I hope you enjoyed *Darkest*.

Pitchblack is the next book in the Boyne Club Series.

Read Rian and Willow's story.

You can download HERE:

https://author-vicarter.com/products/pitchblack

Or read on for a sneak peek:

PITCHBLACK

CHAPTER ONE

Two doors face me. They are wooden, polished, and I know they are heavy in my hands as I have drawn them back many times before. They are pretty harmless. They are, after all, just doors made from wood. I fidget with the pleated skirt that skims my knees.

If they are so harmless, why are you hesitating, Willow?

I'm unsteady as I draw the doors back and step into the room that is my stepbrother's domain. The green wallpaper, with its golden diamond-shaped pattern, gives the room an almost pleasant feel. That is, until you take in the large paintings that are placed around the room. To me, the images look like someone took buckets of paint and splashed them across a canvas. People declare these a masterpiece; I don't.

My gaze darts to Rian as he steps out from behind a dark wooden partition that covers half the room. Blood drips from his fingers and

215

splashes onto the oak flooring. I hold my head up high, and my arms cross tightly behind my back. I hope the beat of my heart isn't penetrating through my blouse and cardigan.

His moss-green eyes smile at me. Shivers skitter down my spine. Rian reaches behind the partition and brings out a white towel that he uses to wipe off the blood from his fingers. It should bother me, the amount of blood, but my brain refuses to acknowledge what's right in front of it. I think it's my brain's way of protecting me.

"Willow." My name from his lips always sends fear pulsing through me along with something else, which I immediately push away.

"Your father asked me to find you." I can't look away as he takes controlled steps towards me. He continues to rub his hands on the cloth. His gray shirt sleeves are rolled up to his elbows. The closer he gets, the more blood I spot — flecks of blood coat his tattooed neck. My heart continues to hammer in my chest. It's right there on the tip of my tongue: the question I want to ask, but I don't—whose blood is coating your arms?

This is my world now. I might not like it, but I can't question it.

Rian steps up to me with only a foot separating us. He's taller, making me feel smaller than my actual five-foot seven-inch frame.

"Why couldn't he come himself?" Rian's words are distracted as he picks up one of my blonde curls in his bloodied fingers and rubs it softly. "Or maybe you wanted to see me."

His moss-green eyes flicker to mine, and that mocking smile he seems to reserve for me spreads across his face. More shivers assault my body as I step away from his touch. He releases my hair, but not before I see his bloody fingerprints on the strands.

"It's my mother's birthday; he wants to make sure you're present."

Rian flashes me another smile and steps towards me again. His fingers are covered in rings, gold rings that are coated in someone's blood. My gaze flickers to the partition, and my pulse spikes. Is the person dead? Are they lying in a pool of their blood? What had they done to deserve such a fate?

Warm, strong fingers grip my chin, drawing me back.

The heat from his fingers burns through my skin, and heat races through me all the way to the tip of my ears. My body feels like it's going to catch on fire from how he is looking at me. I'm ready to ask him to let me go; I'm even willing to ask him nicely when he leans in and sniffs me.

"I'd like to fuck you."

His words are designed to have my mind scattering, and it has the desired effect. I want to run away from him. He's vulgar and a maniac. Yet, I'm still standing here, with blood in my hair and his hands on my face.

"I'll pray for you," I tell him and step out of his touch again. My nostrils flare as I grapple for air. I hate the effect he has on me. It doesn't matter how little or often I'm around him; I can never seem to keep it together. And he knows the effect he has on me.

He grins. It's quick. Rian returns to drying the blood from his hands.

"I can picture you, Willow, on your knees..."

I cut him off as my face blazes. It shouldn't. I should be used to Rian's foul mouth at this stage, but he always has a way of penetrating all my armor, no matter how heavily I put it on.

"Seven o'clock. Don't be late."

I turn, and each step takes a lot of force to keep me upright. No one speaks to Rian like that, but for some reason, he lets me. He knows my fear of him, yet he lets me, just like he taunts me with his foul mouth and dark promises.

My body has cooled down long after I've returned to my bedroom. I move past the large four-poster bed that's been neatly made. The red bed covers are the only color in my whiteout room. My mother hates color, and each time she enters my room, her gaze always zooms to the bed, and her lips curl in distaste.

I enter my bathroom that's also decorated in all white. Here I didn't get to add color. The water turns pink as I wash the blood from my hair. I can't meet my eyes in the mirror. I don't want to see what reflects in them. My fingers tighten around the cold porcelain sink as I close my eyes and take calming breaths.

My heart skips a beat as I look up and meet my eyes in the mirror, and I watch as my control fades. Pushing away from the sink, the feeling of sand slipping through my fingers has me wiping my hands repeatedly on my skirt. I want to bite the flesh of my palms to make the deeply-rooted itch leave.

"Willow." My mother's soft voice is a whip that has me standing straight and stepping into my bedroom. Her gaze skims across my structure before she steps up to me. Her fingers reach out and fix the silver cross that dangles from around my neck.

"You look perfect." She flashes me a wide smile and steps back. Pride shines in her brown eyes, the same color as mine. My mother's blonde hair sits perfectly on her slim shoulders. People say I'm a carbon copy of her. On the outside, I'm sure I am. Inside, I feel like I'm rotten to the core. Black as ink that reflects more darkness. A darkness that I can never let anyone see. She knows I have it in me. She knows what happens when it's let out. So I let her control the darkness in me. If that means being a good Catholic girl, then that's what I will be.

It's not easy living in a place so coated in sin that it's dripping all over everything. But for my mother, I have to try. Rian tests my restraints, but what we lost and how far we've come is a stark reminder to stay on this path.

"Thank you, mother." I smile sweetly, and her smile widens.

"I'm the luckiest woman alive." My mother leaves my room, and I follow. "I have the best daughter." My mother stops and touches my face; I hold still as she caresses it. "And the best husband."

I don't blink until she releases my face, and we make our way down the left staircase. Tonight is a private party for my mother—just the four of us. Tomorrow night, this house will be alive with the elite of our neighborhood.

We enter the foyer. The space is buzzing with life. Florists arrive with large bouquets of flowers and huge plants that graze the top of the front double door frame.

Mark, our party planner, directs every one. Caterers arrive with so much food that it looks like it could feed an army.

"How many people are coming?" I ask as my mother walks through the chaos.

"One hundred and fifty guests. A small gathering. You know I don't like anyone making a fuss over me." My mother pauses and stops a lady from entering the kitchen.

"Don't bring that plant through my kitchen. It smells funny. Bring it out the back."

The lady is ready to leave, but my mother stops her again.

"Actually, take it away. I don't want it."

219

There is a moment when the florist's gaze ping pongs between my mother and me. I have no idea why she is looking at me. She finally nods and leaves with the offending plant.

"Mark." My mother signals Mark with two fingers, beckoning him forward.

I glance down at the large white tile I'm standing on. It's large enough that both my shoes fit into the square. The black polished shoes reflect my face. Feet move around me as my mother makes it clear to Mark that no plants with any type of odor may enter through the kitchen.

I want to exhale loudly or jump up and down, just do something that allows my stiff body to move. The familiar click of his shoes has my head snapping up. But I don't look in Rian's direction. My mother's stance shifts slightly. She's aware of him, too, yet she keeps speaking to Mark.

"Catherine." Rian's voice has that sing-song tone to it that's dipped in annoyance like he's about to hand out his final warning.

I don't direct my attention to Rian. He's to my left. I'm aware of the space he fills. I'm aware of his smell.

Too aware! My brain screams.

"Yes, Rian." My mothers' dislike for him is evident in her tone. When I glance at my mother, she wears a perfectly practiced smile. Mark leaves and orders anyone with plants to go outside for an odor test.

"The noise level, Catherine, is distracting me from my work."

Work!? He means hurting people.

"I'll tell them to keep it down." My mother raises a brow in question. "Anything else?"

I want to look at Rian. I want to see the expression on his face, but I glance around at all the moving bodies. A man carries a crate of wine. I don't drink alcohol. I've often thought about stealing a bottle and letting go, but letting go is dangerous for a person like me.

"No, Catherine." Rian shifts, and some part of me breathes at the expectation of his departure.

He doesn't leave, and when I give in to the urge to look at him, he's staring at me. The gray shirt he wore has been replaced with a dark purple one. Moss-green eyes bore into me, and I'm frozen while being dragged into the vortex of Rian.

He never says anything inappropriate in front of our parents. I honestly don't think it's because he cares what they would say. I think he does it for me. My cheeks blaze at my stupid analysis.

"Willow." I tighten my hands into fists and give him one of my own perfectly practiced smiles. It sits in my inventory for moments, just like this—moments where my mother is watching my reaction.

"Rian," I speak his name clearly.

His lip tugs up before he turns on his heel. Everyone parts like a wave to let him walk through. He doesn't have to pause in his footing or ask anyone to move. It's like everything is repelled by him.

"Willow." My mother is waiting for me, expectantly.

I've been watching Rian for far too long. I give her a softer smile, and she says no more as I follow her to the ballroom where the party will be held tomorrow night.

I sit on a lone chair to the left of the large room as my mother instructs everyone on what she wants to be done. My two feet are firmly on the oak floor, my hands in my lap, and my back straight. This is what keeps everything in me at bay. This is the discipline that will help me keep control. These are my mother's words.

I will sit here for hours and try to blink as little as possible. Every once in a while, my mother will glance at me and give me a nod of approval. I want her approval because each time I get that nod, it's like it restarts my clock, and I'm ready for another hour. I'm aware of how the staff steals glances at me, and like a battery-operated toy, I smile at them on cue.

Download and read HERE:
https://author-vicarter.com/products/pitchblack
Or scan the code below:

OTHER BOOKS BY VI CARTER

THE CELLS OF KALASHOV

THE COLLECTOR #1

THE SIXTH #2

THE HANDLER #3

MURPHY'S MAFIA MADE MEN

SINNER'S VOW #1

SAVAGE MARRIAGE #2

SCANDALOUS PLEDGE #3

SONS OF THE MAFIA

SINS OF THE MAFIA #0.5

VENGEANCE IN BLOOD #1

YOUNG IRISH REBELS SERIES

MAFIA PRINCE #1

MAFIA KING #2

MAFIA GAMES #3

MAFIA BOSS #4

MAFIA SECRETS #5 (NOVELLA)

WILD IRISH SERIES

FATHER (PREQUEL)

VICIOUS #1

RECKLESS #2

RUTHLESS #3

FEARLESS #4

HEARTLESS #5

THE BOYNE CLUB

DARK #1

DARKER # 2

DARKEST #3

PITCH BLACK #4

THE OBSESSED DUET

A DEADLY OBSESSION #1

A CRUEL CONFESSION #2

BROKEN PEOPLE DUET

BREAK ME #1

SAVE ME #2

ABOUT THE AUTHOR

Vi Carter - the queen of **DARK ROMANCE**, the mistress of suspense, and the high priestess of *PLOT TWISTS*!

When she's not busy crafting tales of the **MAFIA** that'll leave you on the edge of your seat, you can find her baking up a storm, exploring the gorgeous Irish countryside, or spending time with her three little girls.

Vi's Young Irish Rebels series has been praised by readers and can be found in English, Dutch, German, Audible and soon will be available in French.

And let's not forget her two greatest loves: ***coffee and chocolate***. If you ever need to bribe her, just offer up a mug of coffee and a slab of chocolate, and she'll be putty in your hands.

So, if you're ready to join Vi on a wild journey with the mafia, sign up for her newsletter and score a free book! Just be warned - her stories are so **ADDICTIVE**, you might not be able to put them down.

What Readers Are Saying

Editorial Reviews

"Vi Carter has once again blown my mind with another outstanding story. She never fails to create a masterpiece with memorable characters that leap off the page. This book is complete perfection."- USA Today Bestselling Author Khardine Gray

Vi is one of those authors who never disappoints. She weaves **LOVE** & **DANGER** effortlessly. ★★★★★ stars

I definitely recommend this book. It is **SUSPENSEFUL** and exciting. I enjoy reading Vi Carter's book. ★★★★★ stars

How to Keep in Touch with Vi Carter
Visit Vi's website: https://author-vicarter.com/
Join the newsletter: t.ly/yZWbX
Or scan the code below:

DARKEST

On Facebook, Instagram, TikTok and YouTube @darkauthorvicarter and
on Twitter @authorvicarter
Or scan the code below:

Milton Keynes UK
Ingram Content Group UK Ltd.
UKHW012049260524
443218UK00001BA/44

9 781915 878502